Lacey
An American Adventure

Cheryl OBrien

Cheryl OBrien

Copyright © 2014 Cheryl OBrien

All rights reserved.

ISBN-10: 1499273274
ISBN-13: 978-1499273274

DEDICATION

This book is dedicated to our ancestors who came from other lands to find a future as Americans. They came to find a place of hope and restoration. They struggled to fit in and to find work. I am blessed to be an American because someone came from Italy to be a citizen of this nation and someone came from Scotland to be a citizen of this nation and someone came from England to be a citizen of this nation. Many of you have a heritage of brave and brilliant people who suffered so that you could live in this America. Treat America well and do something today that will make a difference for the good of an American.

ACKNOWLEDGMENTS

Mark 11:23-26

Jesus answered

I tell you the truth, if anyone says to this mountain, "Go throw yourself into the sea", and does not doubt in his heart but believes that what he says will happen, **it will be done for him**. Therefore I tell you, whatever you ask for in prayer, believe that you have received it and it will be yours. And when you stand praying, if you hold anything against anyone, **forgive** him, so that your Father in heaven may forgive you your sins.

Lacey

Chapter One

"Dear, why didn't Michael choose a ship that would take a direct route to America?" Aunt Mae asked my mother.

"Don't worry Aunt Mae, we will get to America." My mother assured her.

My father joined us a few minutes later with my brother Ethan.

"Aunty Mae, many people have made this trip to America. We will be fine. I have enough money for us once we get there and I can find a job as a carpenter. Don't worry about us." My father told her.

Aunt Mae kissed my mother and me on the cheek and hugged my father and my older brother Ethan before we boarded the ship. We watched her wave to us as the ship pulled out of the harbor. Then my father found out where we would be sleeping. Our tickets were numbered according to the bunk our family would share. We had to go down a steep ladder and we were not prepared for the reality of our accommodations. We were sharing a room with so many others. Large wooden bunk beds were stacked all along the walls. There was a section to keep our ration of food that included oatmeal, flour, eggs, and other food elements that would survive the trip. Water was also rationed. My mother looked worried.

"We will be fine Clarice. I arranged for a double portion when I bought the tickets." He checked our supplies and he had received what he paid for.

"Michael, there isn't much privacy here." My mother said.

"We will hold up our blankets for privacy and be careful to respect the privacy of others. One of the crew suggested that you and Lacey keep your bonnets on during the voyage, especially down here. There have been problems with lice before so we must be careful. Ethan will watch over Lacey and I will watch over you. You and Lacey are never to go anywhere unescorted."

"I will protect Lacey, Mother, don't worry." Ethan assured her.

"If you two are on deck then your mother and I will watch over our supplies. When we want to go up, you and Ethan watch over our supplies." My father told us.

"Yes Sir." Ethan agreed.

Despite the inconvenience of our accommodations my father remained excited to start a new free life in America. He had high hopes for success. During the first few days at sea my parents spoke with many of the passengers while my older brother kept a watchful eye on me. Ethan was very protective and pulled me away from every young man who seemed interested in saying hello to me.

"Ethan, please don't pull me around like that. It's embarrassing and humiliating. I resent being handled." I argued.

"This is a long voyage. I will not have you become the prey of any of the young men on this ship." He sounded like he was angry with me.

"I have not done anything wrong. All I am asking you to do is be gentler about moving me along. The word gentleman suggests that there is gentleness involved." I was determined to make my point.

"Fine. I will not yank you around as long as you move away willingly." He agreed.

"Thank you." I smiled at him.

"Sir, could you help me with something?" A pretty young lady got my brother's attention.

He tipped his hat toward her. "It would be my pleasure, Miss. My name is Ethan Dopolis and this is my sister, Lacey."

"Pleased to meet you both. My name is Tricia Stamos. Please come with me." She started to explain as we walked. "We were sitting on the deck on one of the benches when it became dislodged. My brother is trying to fix it but with the boat rocking back and forth he can't hold it in place and I am simply not strong enough. He sent me to find help." She explained.

We followed her to the bench. Her brother was holding it in place, but he couldn't do that and fix it at the same time. Ethan worked with him to secure the bench to the deck.

"It won't move now." Ethan told him.

"Ethan and Lacey Dopolis, this is my brother Kurt Stamos." Tricia introduced us.

Ethan shook his hand. This seemed like the first break for

me to be able to meet people who were close to our age.

"Glad I could help." Ethan smiled at Tricia.

"We didn't want to cause trouble on the ship." Kurt explained. "My father and I saved for years trying to buy passage for us. We are going to America to live with relatives in Boston, Massachusetts until we get settled. I hate being crammed in below deck. I am assuming you are on the opposite side of the ship. We haven't seen you near the bunks in our section." Kurt said.

"We are toward the middle against the wall on the top bunk." Ethan told him.

"We are more toward the front of the ship on the bottom. Tricia hates it there. The ship moves too much for her to relax." Kurt explained.

"Thank you for your help. I know our time is limited up here and we didn't want to make anyone angry and be punished with having to stay off the deck." Tricia said.

Ethan spoke with Kurt while I visited with Tricia. Even though Ethan was interested in speaking with Tricia, he was careful not to give that impression to Kurt. He didn't want him to pull her away from us. While the two of them spoke Tricia and I started to walk the deck. Our brothers followed to keep a close eye on us.

At supper time we invited the Stamos family to sit with our family and share the oatmeal that was provided for us as part of our ticket. Ethan and I were never very hungry because of the rocking of the ship. We watched as our parents got along well with the Stamos family.

"I never thought the day would come that I would share a bunk with both parents and my sister." Kurt said.

"That is not what I mind so much. It is being crammed in between rows of families we don't know and all the snoring. I've kept this bonnet on for nearly the entire voyage so far. I'm afraid of getting lice in my hair." I told him.

"You have beautiful hair Lacey. Keep the bonnet on. It is worth it. Working on a ship is much different than being a passenger. At least with working I've spent most of my time in the open air." He said.

Just then we saw a rat run by us. I jumped. "I hate those things. This is so much worse than I imagined." I told him.

"Lacey, relax. I've seen where your family is sleeping. You are high enough to be away from them in your bunk. You really have the best section." Kurt told me. "Your parents must have had a little bit of money to arrange for that bunk."

During the next four days we were inseparable. Because Ethan was interested in speaking with Tricia and Kurt was interested in speaking with me, the two brothers compromised. They agreed that as long as the four of us stayed close to each other, they would relax their overbearing behavior.

"Lacey, do you mind if I ask you your age?" Kurt asked me.

"Tell me your age first and I will tell you approximately how close I am to it." I bargained.

"Twenty-four", he answered.

"You look older, but that could be because you are tall and you look very strong. Ethan is twenty-two and I am younger than him." I told him.

"Well, Tricia is eighteen. Are you younger than my sister?" He asked me.

"Do I look younger?" I asked.

He smiled. "So this inquiry does bother you?"

"I am considered to be an adult." I told him.

"By what standard?" He asked.

"You're fresh Mr. Stamos." I found his argument amusing.

"I was just concerned that you might become a spinster if someone did not offer you a marriage proposal soon." He joked.

"That would seem an insulting comment, but I refuse to be insulted. I think your words have given me a clear observation of your inabilities. Could it be that you need glasses?" I teased.

"I have perfect vision, but apparently not perfect manners. My apologies Miss Lacey. Would you be willing to tell me why you are not here with a husband?"

"The right man has not asked for my hand yet. I would prefer remaining single to the possibility of marrying the wrong man." I told him as we walked along the deck.

"Have you had offers of marriage?" He asked me.

"Twice." I admitted.

Just then a fight broke out on deck between two men. Cooking food was an issue on board. There were many passengers and not enough room or time for everyone to prepare their own meal.

"Let the crew handle it. That is what they get paid for." Kurt said as he showed me how to avoid the people involved. "So you were saying you've been proposed to twice. What were some of your reasons for refusing the proposals?" He asked me.

"Well the first offer I got was from a young man of merely seven years old. I thought he was much too young for me, even though I was nine at the time."

"Wise decision and the other offer?" He asked.

"We were moving to America and he was not. I didn't want to fall in love with him and then have to leave him. We knew each other for a short time and then he decided to ask the question." I told him.

"Was he very disappointed that you turned him down?" Kurt asked.

"He was surprised by my answer. He had money and position and thought that was enough. He told me I was foolish to turn down such an attractive offer." I told him.

"So money doesn't impress you?" Kurt asked.

"It is the character of the man that impresses me. God can

make a pauper rich in a day with just his favor and grace. I trust that the man I should be with will be revealed to me in time." I told him.

"And what do you think of me?" He asked.

"I have no great opinion of you yet. I don't know you very well at all." I told him.

"That's fair." He smiled.

"So tell me about yourself." I suggested.

"I'm pleasant and considerate. I work hard when I work. I've worked mostly on ships. I've had many occupations in regard to the sea. I love the excitement and the peace of the ocean. We heard that Boston, Massachusetts would be a good harbor to find work. It will take us a little longer to get there, but I believe my parents want to live near there." He told me.

"Did you go out in the morning and come back at night when you were working on the ship?" I asked him.

"Not always. Sometimes we spent days at sea, the crew and I. Rough water doesn't bother me like some of the people on this ship. My sister doesn't care for the rocking. She needs fresh air when that is happening."

Just after sunrise the next morning we heard warnings from the crew to stay in our bunks. A storm was approaching the ship. The seas became increasingly violent. Many on board were concerned for our safety. As the smell of the living area below deck became too much to bear I begged my parents to allow me to go up on deck to get some air. I promised them that I would tie myself to the ship. My father gave in only after Ethan guaranteed that he would tie himself to me and watch over me. We met Kurt and Tricia as they made their way up the ladder to the upper deck.

"It looks like you two have the same idea. It is a nasty smell below. Tricia cannot stomach it." Kurt told us.

Kurt and Ethan grabbed for the thin rope that was hanging on a hook as we approached the door that led out to the deck.

"It is safer if we borrow this rope and tie ourselves together. We don't know what we will be facing on deck." Ethan said.

"Ethan, tie the end of the rope to your wrist. Then we will tie the girls and I will tie myself last. When we get on deck we will secure the extra rope to the ship and try to stand back against the wall of the ship. Hold Lacey tight. I'll hold on to Tricia." Kurt instructed.

"Why are you leaving so much length between us?" I asked my brother.

"If you should get swept overboard you will take me with you. I want room to swim and a length of rope to pull you back to me." He answered.

"Do you really think that might happen?" I was worried.

"It's possible. I'll hold on to you and you stay close." Ethan said.

Our desperation for fresh air forced us on to the deck. I was surprised by how many people had the same idea and no rope. The crew was not happy about the number of people struggling to stay on deck during the storm. We watched as the crew fought to secure the ship and keep it on course.

Then we all saw it at once, a large wave that was headed for the ship.

"Ethan!" Kurt yelled. "Cut us away from the ship or we will sink with it!"

"No!" Ethan yelled. "The ship will survive this."

"We will die! Cut the rope!" Kurt yelled.

Ethan refused and Kurt hit him hard in the face. Then he cut the rope himself and picked Ethan up. "Dive in girls or he will take you with him."

I begged him with the few seconds I had, not to throw my brother into the water.

"I'm saving us." He shouted as he threw him into the water. He picked me up next and then Tricia. It took seconds and we were all overboard. Ethan hit the water and came to himself.

"Swim Lacey! Swim away from the ship!" He yelled to me.

The four of us swam as fast as we could in fear that the wave would hit the ship and throw it into us. It was a miracle that did not happen. We missed one wave but got taken under by another. When we came up Tricia and I were struggling because we had gotten tangled in the rope and our dresses and shoes felt like weights.

"Calm down!" Kurt yelled. He held on to Tricia and was

able to pull the rope away from her.

Ethan helped me. I was grateful both men were strong.

"Pull off your shoes." Kurt ordered us.

Ethan looked back at the ship and saw it sinking. He realized Kurt was right. He got hold of my feet and removed my shoes as Kurt took off Tricia's shoes. Then they removed their own. We continued to go under and come up again as the waves rushed over us.

"Ethan you have to cut the length of Lacey's dress. The weight of it will cause her to drown." Kurt yelled to him.

Ethan obeyed and was careful to take his knife out of the holder attached to his belt. He cut at my dress and left me nothing below my knees and shredded most of the rest of it. Kurt took care to cut away most of the length of Tricia's dress too.

Then each of them secured their knives in the knife holder attached to their belts while they struggled to stay above water.

We were relieved that we felt lighter in the water, but worried about being exposed by the new length of our dresses. The waves were still tossing us, but Kurt and Ethan were very strong and able to keep us from drowning. Kurt instructed all of us as we stayed together trying to survive the storm. I don't even know how we were able to survive it, but we did. When the storm passed we were still tied together.

"I'm going to cut the rope." Kurt told us. "We need to rest and the only way to do that is to take turns floating. We can't do that tied together like we are."

We trusted him. Ethan helped him cut the rope. Then he spotted some barrels floating in the water. "Kurt, look over there." He pointed.

"They must be from the ship. Let's get them." Kurt led the way as we swam toward the barrels. He reached them first and brought the first one back to Tricia. "Tricia, I'm going to help you to lie across it. It will help you rest. Lacey, hold on to it until I bring one back for you."

We were able to get hold of three of them. We leaned on them and used them to rest on. We saw there was land in the distance. It took us the rest of that day to swim to the island. We made it to shore just before the sun went down. We were exhausted. Tricia and I dragged ourselves away from the water and collapsed on the sand. We just wanted to sleep.

Ethan and Kurt pulled the barrels on to shore and looked around until they found us a place to lie down for the night. Ethan and Kurt collected wood and branches for a fire. It took them a while but they were able to get one started to warm us up. That night I slept next to my brother as he kept his arms around me to keep me warm. Kurt took care of Tricia the same way. In the morning the men were awake first. They opened one of the barrels and found that it had fresh water to drink. That was a welcome surprise. Ethan found us some fruit to eat.

"We have to find shelter first and then food. Each day we will walk further to explore the island. We don't know where we are or what dangers are here so you girls will go nowhere alone. Ethan we need to make some weapons for self defense." Kurt told him.

"What of our clothes?" I asked Ethan as I looked down at our exposed legs. "These dresses are not proper."

"I realize you are wearing less material than you are used to, but Kurt and I agreed that we will treat each of you respectfully. If we can find something else for you to wear, we will do that. Right now we need shelter and food." Ethan said.

"Ethan, what of our parents?" I asked him.

"It is obvious Lacey. They have perished. They are with Jesus now. I would mourn with you, but we don't have time for that luxury right now." Ethan said as he got up to lead the way away from the shoreline.

"Why can't we stay here?" I asked him.

"Lacey, it is too open. There is no shelter for us here and we don't know who is on this island. We aren't even sure it is an island. We don't know the environment. We have to explore our options. Be careful where you step. You have no shoes to protect your feet." Kurt warned.

"What about the barrels?" I asked him.

"Once we find a place we can take shelter, I will come back for them." He told us.

We walked about a hundred yards and it was apparent we needed something on our feet and weapons to defend ourselves.

"We should turn back to the beach. We are unprepared for this." I worried.

"Lacey is right. For now we need to come up with something to protect our feet. We should head back to the beach and think about this again." Ethan said.

"There is no reason to go back that far. There is a clearer place ahead. You girls take the time to clear the area as best you can when we get there and Ethan and I will try to build a temporary shelter for us." Kurt headed toward the area as we followed.

Tricia and I moved the branches and rocks we could lift out of the area Kurt had picked out. We piled the branches to the side to use for a fire later. The men started to look around for anything they could use to build us a shelter.

"Ethan, look there!" I pointed toward the hillside to the east. There was white smoke.

"What do you think?" He asked Kurt.

"The trees are too thick to see where it is coming from, but it's not black so it is not the forest that is on fire. It looks like we have company." Kurt said.

"How far away do you think that is?" Ethan asked him.

"Could be as much as a day's walk, more without shoes." He guessed.

"We should build a fire of our own and let them know we are here." Tricia suggested.

"No, we shouldn't. We don't know who it is or what they are doing here. We don't want more trouble." Kurt insisted. "We will build a shelter for the night, no fire. We will just have to sleep closer together. You girls in the middle next to each other and Ethan and I will stay on each side."

"He's right. We have a lot to do today." Ethan said.

"What about food and water?" I asked him.

"We have to get one of the barrels and bring it closer. Then we will get you girls some fruit, but first shelter. Clear the area." Ethan ordered. "If you find any stones with a sharp edge, give them to me."

Tricia and I were very diligent about clearing the area. We looked around for sharp stones and we were able to find a few that were good size. Ethan had an inventive mind. He fashioned an axe to cut down the thinner trees. Then he made a tomahawk, and spears. Kurt directed Tricia and me to help him build a stone wall as there were many rocks in our area. We were careful to watch for snakes and bugs as we attempted to move them. Kurt was very strong. When Ethan was finished putting together a few weapons, he took a walk back to the beach and carried back one of the barrels.

Ethan took Kurt aside when he got back. "Some of the items from the ship are washing up on shore. There are bodies too. I don't want the girls to come back to that." He whispered.

"I have to finish this. Bring back what you can. If the dead are wearing shoes remove them and bring them back. We need shoes, weapons, clothing, and anything else that will help us survive this." Kurt told him.

"Alright." Ethan left us again. He returned carrying a

trunk on his shoulder. He put it down in front of us and opened it.

"Ethan, this is wonderful. Where did you get it?" I asked him.

"It was floating in the water." He answered. "You girls go through it. I already found myself a pair of shoes to wear. I'm going back for more. I'll be back in a few minutes." Then he left us again.

"Tricia, we should hang these up to dry in the sun." I told her of the items in the trunk.

"Lacey, have Tricia do that alone. I need your help with these stones." Kurt told me. "If there are shoes in that trunk put them on your feet first. If you find a pair for me, bring them here."

I did what he instructed me to do. Ten minutes later Ethan was back with another load of items. He took the empty trunk back with him to fill it again. He made eight trips back and forth from the beach. Among the items were coats, blankets, clothing, combs and barrettes, shoes, and a few more knives and some wine bottles. Kurt was grateful that we found a corkscrew in the trunk.

"Did you do anything with the bodies?" Kurt asked him privately.

"Not yet, but I think it would be a good idea to bury them or burn them." Ethan suggested.

"Let's sleep on it and just keep the girls away from the beach for now." Kurt told him.

"We need to eat. I'll go collect what I can for food." Ethan told him. He left us and returned thirty minutes later with bananas and coconuts.

After we ate and had some water to drink we continued to work on our shelter. The sun was hot so the clothing we had laid out dried quickly. Tricia and I changed our clothes while the men were working.

"Ethan, if there is someone else on the island they might be a danger to the girls." Kurt suggested.

"We will have to protect them." Ethan said as he lifted another rock.

"Remember the story in the bible about Abraham and Sarah? Remember when Abraham told his wife Sarah to say she was his sister and not his wife?" Kurt asked.

"Yeah, what about it." Ethan said.

"I'm suggesting that we protect our sisters by telling whoever we meet that they are our wives." Kurt said.

"Why?" Ethan asked.

"Men think twice about taking another man's wife. They don't use the same logic when it is your sister. I can sleep beside Tricia without a problem and I am sure Lacey doesn't mind sleeping next to you. It is just safer if something happens." He suggested.

"We should tell the girls this plan." Ethan suggested.

"Tricia will just worry about it. Please keep it between us for now. If someone approaches us, then we will tell them."

Kurt whispered as I approached with another rock.

The wall was almost finished on three sides. It was a little over three feet high, made up of stones and branches. Then Kurt and Ethan went about finishing the fourth side with a small entrance for us to climb in through. They put thick branches over the top of the structure and fastened the heavier coats to the branches for a roof. Then they covered the coats with more branches and leaves.

We worked together until the sun went down. Tricia and I spread blankets out on the floor of the shelter. We checked every item for bugs before we brought it into the shelter. Ethan blocked the entrance with the spears he had made to keep the animals out. Kurt blocked the entrance with another blanket. That night Tricia and I slept in the middle and Ethan and Kurt slept appropriately on the ends. It was dark inside and I was sure that Tricia was as frightened as I was to go to sleep. We held on to each other for comfort. Our brothers tried to comfort us by declaring that nothing could get inside. We didn't believe them.

When we finally fell asleep, we slept well.

Chapter Two

Kurt and Ethan went down to the beach in the morning while Tricia and I were sleeping. They expected the bodies to be floating in the water, but they were all gone along with all of the items Ethan had not brought back to us.

"I don't understand this. There is no sign of anything I left here." Ethan looked around in amazement.

"Well, the stuff didn't just walk off. Someone else is living on this island. Let's get back to the girls." Kurt turned to run back to us with Ethan following close behind.

Tricia started to climb out first and she screamed and came back inside. "There are three dark men outside Lacey and our brothers aren't here."

"Young lady, we are here to help, not to hurt. Please come out." His accent was strange to us.

Kurt and Ethan ran to the shelter and got between it and the men.

"Who are you and what do you want?" Kurt asked them.

"My name is Elliot. I am in charge of security on this island. These men help me. Some of the people on the island discovered parts of the wreckage and the bodies late yesterday afternoon. They reported the findings to me. We worked for hours cleaning up the area. This area of the island is owned by Prentice Sheffield. We are here to help you. Mr. Sheffield asked us to look for survivors. I suspect you are the survivors of the wreckage."

"Yes Sir. We were on a ship and got caught in a great storm. It went down taking everyone on board with it. We are the only survivors that we know of. My name is Kurt Stamos and this is Ethan Dopolis."

"And the young ladies?" Elliot asked.

"Tricia Stamos and Lacey Dopolis." Kurt answered.

"Very well. Please tell your wives that it is safe to come out. We have been instructed to take you all to Mr. Sheffield's manor. He is eager to help you." Elliot told us.

"Wives?" I whispered to Tricia.

"Just go along with it Lacey. If Kurt did not correct him, there is a very good reason." Tricia whispered.

We climbed out of the shelter as Ethan pushed the covering aside. He took my left hand and Kurt took Tricia's. They didn't want Elliot to notice that we had no wedding band. We followed Elliot as the other two men walked behind us. We walked down to the beach and then another thirty minutes to a beautiful manor that overlooked the water. It was quite a climb up to the front door of the manor.

Elliot knocked on the door and a butler answered the door.

"Mr. Sheffield is expecting us. Please tell him I found four survivors of the wreckage." Elliot told the butler.

The butler left us at the door and returned a few minutes later. "Mr. Sheffield is in the sitting room. Please follow me."

We entered the sitting room as the butler announced us.

Mr. Sheffield was about fifty years old. He stood up to greet us. He looked like a very pleasant fellow. He smiled as he shook Kurt's hand and then Ethan's.

"It is a pleasure to meet all of you. My name is Prentice Sheffield. I retired to this island some years ago with my wife, Judith. She passed away two years ago and that left me to enjoy my retirement alone. I am so glad that you survived. I am sure that you have lots to share with me, but first I would like you to be my guests and take advantage of my hospitality. How can I arrange your rooms for you? I have eight for you to choose from." He said quite cheerfully.

Kurt and Ethan started to relax.

"Thank you for your kindness, Mr. Sheffield. Your man Elliot was under the impression that we were married to these lovely ladies, however, they are our sisters. This is Ethan Dopolis and his sister Lacey. I am Kurt Stamos and this is my sister Tricia. Whatever accommodations you have available to us, I am sure will be more than adequate." Kurt said.

"Please Mr. Stamos, follow my butler and he will bring you to your rooms. I will send the house servants to your room to provide you with the necessities you will need to refresh yourselves. When you have had a chance to refresh yourselves and change, please join me here and I will see that you are provided food." Mr. Sheffield instructed graciously. "My butler will inform you where you can find all that you need to make your stay with us a pleasant one."

"Thank you Sir," was the reply from all of us before we left to follow the butler upstairs to the bedrooms.

As we walked up the staircase the butler inquired of our sizes. He was very considerate to show Tricia and me our rooms last so he could ask those particular questions with some privacy. The plan was that while we were bathing he would send someone to get clothing for us.

"Very nice young people Elliot. Thank you for bringing them here." Mr. Sheffield smiled.

"You're welcome, Sir. If I can be of future assistance, please call on me." Elliot responded. Then he shook Mr. Sheffield's hand and left with his two men.

After my bath was ready, I locked my door and stepped into the clean water. I sat back in the tub and started to wash when I was overcome by tears of relief at being rescued and tears of sorrow at the loss of my parents. I could hear Tricia in the next room going through the same emotions.

Kurt and Ethan responded quickly to our cries but when they realized we were not in danger they went back inside their rooms without disturbing us.

About an hour later Ethan came to the door of my bedroom and knocked on it. "Lacey, are you ready?"

I came out and took his hand. "I'm ready."

"I heard you crying before." He told me.

"I am better now." I assured him.

He smiled at me. "We will get through this together. I will not abandon you." He kissed me on the cheek.

I smiled at him. "Thank you."

We walked past Kurt as he was on his way to Tricia's room.

"Lacey, are you alright now?" He asked me.

"Yes, thank you for asking. I am fine."

Kurt smiled and went on his way. As we descended the staircase we could hear him knocking on Tricia's door. They entered the sitting room a few moments after us. Mr. Sheffield was not there. His butler entered and directed us up another staircase and outside to the balcony that overlooked the water.

"Such a beautiful sight and it can be so fierce at times. Please sit down and enjoy the food and wine." He invited us as he took his place at the table.

Kurt and Ethan helped us with our chairs and then they sat down next to us.

"This is very kind of you Mr. Sheffield." I said as he passed me a plate of sliced beef.

"It is my pleasure Miss Lacey. I get very few visitors here. I am grateful for your company." He said.

"Are there many inhabitants on this island, Mr. Sheffield?"

Kurt asked.

"Mostly darker colored individuals. My wife and I came here years ago. She found the language intriguing and the people pleasant. Certainly you have noticed the beauty of the island. We needed peace in our lives and I had money to invest into developing the natural resources of this land, so we came back. We had this manor built and I own the only export company on the island." He explained.

"So you have a ship?" Ethan asked.

"Yes Ethan, I have three ships. They take two to three week journeys to deliver my goods to other ports. I hired the captains and the crews from various places. All are very well paid and very diligent to complete their assignments. Business is so good that I am having another ship built. It will be completed in a month or so." He explained.

"Are there other business men like you on the island?" Tricia inquired.

"Yes Miss Tricia. There is Mr. Donovan Cross. He owns a manufacturing company on the island and a restaurant. There is also my friend Benjamin Carlyle. His company actually operates in England, but he and his wife Juliet prefer to live on the island. This is one of the ports he imports his goods to."

"Do you know if Mr. Carlyle is the owner of Carlyle and Son?" I asked him.

"Yes, Miss Lacey he is. Do you know the family?" Mr. Sheffield asked.

"Yes, I know his son Joseph Carlyle." I told him.

"Oh now I understand. You are the woman who broke Joseph's heart. I heard wonderful things about you, Miss Lacey. It certainly is a small world." Mr. Sheffield smiled.

"Excuse me Mr. Sheffield, but how would you have heard about me?" I asked him.

"I met Joseph just the other day. He spoke of a beautiful woman named Lacey. He told me that your family had left for America and taken you with them. He was quite sorrowful about your departure. He is on the island visiting his parents." Mr. Sheffield informed me. "Should I contact him and tell him that you are staying here?"

"Please don't trouble yourself Mr. Sheffield." I said politely.

"Nonsense Miss Lacey, it is no trouble at all." He called his butler over. "Milton, send someone to the Carlyle house and inform them of the rescue situation. Invite them to join us for the supper meal at six o'clock tonight to meet the survivors."

"Yes Sir, Mr. Sheffield." Milton left immediately.

We were all surprised by the speed with which Mr. Sheffield moved to inform Joseph and his family of our arrival.

Everyone went on eating and conversing. Mr. Sheffield invited us to enjoy his home and explore the property freely. He was a gracious host.

"Please excuse me." He said as he left the table. "I have business to attend to. Supper will be at six. Your formal clothes will be provided you for the supper meal."

"Thank you, Mr. Sheffield." We all replied.

He smiled and left us. Then Kurt got up from his chair. "Miss Lacey, would you like to go for a walk on the beach with me?" He asked.

I looked at Ethan for his approval. He gave it. I got up from my chair and took Kurt's hand. We walked down to the beach together, leaving Tricia and Ethan alone to talk.

"This Joseph Carlyle fellow is the one who asked you to marry him?" Kurt asked.

"Yes." I answered.

"Did you love him?" Kurt asked.

"I already answered that question. I knew my parents had planned on moving us to America. I did not allow myself to love Joseph. He was very kind to me. I think you might like him. His only true fault is his money and the belief that having it gives him more power over people than it actually does." I told him.

"If your parents hadn't planned to move to America would you have married him?" Kurt asked.

"When will you give this up?" I asked him.

"Lacey, I have feelings for you. I just want to know if Mr. Joseph Carlyle has a chance with you. I would like to know if you might be open to having a relationship with me?" He asked.

"I am a single young woman. I am not committed to anyone. I don't want to play games with either of you. We don't know each other very well." I reminded him.

"All I ask is that you be fair to us." Kurt said.

"Kurt, please understand that this is not a competition for my affection. I knew Joseph for a few months and during that time he was very busy. He claimed he was sure that he loved me, but I'm not sure of that. What I am sure of is that two months was not enough time for me to commit myself to him. I couldn't give up on living in America. I wanted that. Ethan and I still want that." I told him.

"I understand." He continued to walk with me and talk to me.

"I suppose my brother is interested in your sister." Tricia told Ethan as they walked around the outside of the manor.

"He is a nice guy. I think he would be good for Lacey." Ethan said.

"Did you approve of this Joseph fellow?" Tricia asked.

"He was nice enough, but he seemed to be under his father's thumb." Ethan answered.

"In what way?" Tricia asked.

"Are you going to talk about others all afternoon, or talk about us?" Ethan asked.

"What about us?" Tricia asked.

"You're beautiful and intelligent Tricia. I like being around you. Do you see me in your future?" He asked.

"Yes, I think we could be very good friends." She smiled.

"Friends only?" He seemed disappointed.

She surprised him by kissing him on the lips, which he was quick to respond to.

"Your brother would have my head if he saw us." Ethan smiled.

"My brother wants to do that very thing with your sister. Fair is fair." She replied as she leaned back against the outside wall of the manor.

Ethan looked around to make sure they were not in danger of being spotted then he kissed her again, longer this time.

She smiled when he stopped. "Quite impressive Mr. Dopolis, but don't get the wrong idea about me. I am impatient, not promiscuous."

"You are a delight Tricia." He went to kiss her again.

She pushed him back gently. "I think we should do a little more talking and a lot less kissing."

"And why is that?" Ethan asked her.

"Because my brother and your sister are approaching and Kurt has a few more muscles than you do." She smiled.

Ethan looked behind him. "Thank you for saving me from a bashing." Then he looked back at her. "I am intrigued by you Tricia. We will continue our discussion later."

She smiled as she moved away from the wall and started walking to meet us.

Chapter Three

That evening we dressed for the supper meal. The men waited for us in the dining room with Mr. Sheffield. A few minutes before six o'clock the Carlyle family was escorted to the dining room. They greeted Mr. Sheffield politely. Joseph controlled his exuberance at the sight of my brother.

"Is Lacey with you?" He asked Ethan.

"Yes Joseph, she survived the ship with us. She will be here in a few moments." Ethan told him.

I entered the room with Tricia. Joseph was quick to come to me.

"Lacey." He hugged me. "I'm sorry, but my joy at seeing you has overwhelmed me." He said as he stood back.

"It's alright Joseph. I am happy to see you too. This is my friend Tricia Stamos." I introduced her.

"So pleased to meet you Miss Tricia." Joseph smiled.

"It is a pleasure to meet you too, Mr. Carlyle." Tricia replied.

"Please, call me Joseph." He smiled at her.

"Please everyone, find a comfortable seat." Mr. Sheffield directed us.

We sat down to enjoy the meal Mr. Sheffield had provided for all of us.

"Lacey, it is such a pleasure to meet you." Mrs. Carlyle said. "Joseph had tried to describe you to us, but his description seems vague now that we've seen you in person. I can understand why my son referred to you as beautiful."

"You are most kind, Mrs. Carlyle." I responded.

"What happened to the ship?" Mr. Carlyle asked.

"It went down in a storm. We lost our parents as did Ethan and Lacey." Kurt replied. "If you don't mind Mr. Carlyle, that subject still upsets my sister. Could we speak of more pleasant things?"

"Of course. My apologies to you all. I'm very sorry for your loss." He went back to eating his meal.

"We were grateful that Mr. Sheffield sent someone to find us. He has been so generous with his hospitality." I smiled at Mr. Sheffield.

"Your smile lights up the room, Lacey." Mr. Sheffield patted my hand. "You are welcome to stay here as my guests for as long as you like." Then he turned to his other guests. "I have been lonely here since my wife died. The sound of others talking inside these walls brings me great joy."

"The meal is delicious Mr. Sheffield." Ethan remarked.

The others agreed as they ate.

"I have one of the best cooks on the island. I would rather have a good meal and fine company than all the gold in the world. Riches do not buy happiness." Mr. Sheffield remarked.

"Quite true. Lacey could not be persuaded by my wealth. I think that is why I fell in love with her so quickly." Joseph looked at me lovingly.

I put my head down from the embarrassment of his words.

Kurt was irritated that Joseph had made me uncomfortable. He decided to change the subject. "My sister and I still desire to find a way to America. How about you Ethan? Have you thought about continuing our voyage on another ship?" He asked.

"I know Lacey has her heart set on going to America. My parents desired us to experience the hope of a new place. I think we owe it to their memory to find a way to continue the journey." Ethan replied.

"This is a new place for you. Maybe it was fate that brought you here. May I suggest that you take some time to check out the island? You may come to love it here." Mr. Carlyle offered.

"I would welcome you extending your stay here." Mr. Sheffield said.

Kurt smiled. "I'm sure we will talk about your suggestion. We realize that with nothing in our pockets buying passage at this time would be difficult. Ethan and I must find employment soon."

We spent another hour with the Carlyle family. Joseph

took the time to speak with Kurt and Ethan. There was no doubt that they enjoyed the conversation. After our guests had left Mr. Sheffield excused himself and went into the library to relax with a book. Ethan invited Tricia to walk with him in the moonlight while Kurt invited me back to the balcony for some fresh air.

"I like your friend Joseph. He is smart and entertaining." Kurt said as we walked to the edge of the balcony.

"I love the view from here and the sound of the waves." I told him.

He spotted Ethan kissing Tricia. "Is that why he invited her to walk with him?" He seemed upset.

I thought he was going to leave me and go punch my brother. I grabbed his sleeve. "It is beautiful here and the moon is so bright. Let Tricia enjoy the romance of the evening." I whispered.

"It is a brother's duty to protect his sister." Kurt replied.

I covered his eyes with my hands. "Don't look. Tricia won't allow Ethan to do anything wrong and Ethan cares about your sister. He doesn't want to upset her. You have nothing to worry about." I removed my hands.

He smiled at me. "They are distracting me. The real reason I am upset is because we have not shared a kiss. I want to kiss you Lacey."

"Not tonight Kurt. I would feel like we were doing it because I owed it to you after watching Ethan and Tricia. If we do share a kiss and I am not saying that we will, I would want it to be just between us; not because of them and not because of Joseph." I explained.

"I understand completely. We've been through so much in such a short time. The four of us should take the time to discuss what our short term plans are for the future. Do you think you might want to stay on the island for a while?" He asked.

"I'm not sure. To be honest I'm a little frightened of getting on a ship again, especially without you. You were responsible for saving our lives. You know so much about ships and the ocean. I know that I don't want to leave without you. I wouldn't feel safe." I admitted.

"I appreciate your confidence in me. When Tricia and I choose to leave, I will try my best to make arrangements so that you and Ethan can leave with us. I don't mind being a little patient until you make up your mind." Kurt told me.

"Thank you." I put my hand on his as it rested on the stone wall of the balcony.

We spent another hour talking. Ethan and Tricia joined us after that. The four of us discussed going to America. We came up with a plan to speak with Mr. Sheffield the next morning about touring the island.

At breakfast Kurt mentioned it and Mr. Sheffield was happy to give us a guided tour. He arranged for the transportation. We got ready and an hour later we were stepping into a six-seater buggy pulled by four horses. Mr. Sheffield took the middle seat next to me. His driver sat up front with Ethan. Tricia and Kurt had the back seat. Mr.

Sheffield spoke about the island for the entire three hours. We rode through the island on one road and came back to the manor using another. Many times along the way, we stopped and Mr. Sheffield introduced us to the business owners and the people along the way. The trip was quite informative and very entertaining. When we arrived back at the manor I was tired from the journey, but I didn't want to go inside yet. There was too much daylight left to enjoy.

"Ladies, if you would like to rest on the beach I have provided the latest in swimwear for you. You will find bathing suits on your beds and the servants will bring chairs or a blanket down to the beach for you to relax on." Mr. Sheffield said.

"Thank you very much." Tricia and I said at the same time. We were excited to check out the bathing suits. So we ran upstairs to our rooms to check them out.

"Wait Tricia!" Kurt yelled after her.

She turned around at the top of the staircase. "Stop worrying about me. If I don't think it is proper, I won't put it on."

"I assure you Mr. Stamos, it will not be as revealing as the bathing attire you saw this morning on some of the locals. The young ladies are being supplied with bathing suits suitable for swimming and the most modern for the time we are in. New designs for 1820 are coming out daily. If the outfits cause them to smile, please don't say anything to remove the joy from their faces." Mr. Sheffield said. "By the way, your bathing suits are on your beds too."

"Mr. Sheffield, you have been more than generous to us. We really appreciate your kindness." Ethan said.

"I have money and no one I care about to spend it on. Allow an old man the privilege of spoiling you a little. I never had children and if I had you all would be about the age they would have been. I'm enjoying all of this. Enjoy your day. That will bless me." Mr. Sheffield explained.

"We don't know what to say." Ethan responded.

"You don't have to say anything. Please just enjoy yourselves." Mr. Sheffield turned and left Ethan and Kurt standing in the hall.

Tricia came to my room and knocked on the door. "Lacey, I'm dressed. How do you look?" She whispered.

I came out of my room. "I think we both look cute in these. Let's race down to the water before our brothers stop us."

She grabbed my hand and we ran down the hall toward the staircase. We were at the bottom of the stairs when our brothers came out of their rooms and heard us. They knew we were trying to get away with something so they raced to catch up with us. The butler was holding towels for us as we raced through the back door. Tricia and I grabbed one each and yelled a thank you as we ran out the door toward the water. We dropped our towels on the sand and ran into the water and dove in before Ethan or Kurt could stop us.

Mr. Sheffield was watching from the balcony and laughing as our brothers tried to catch up. He stood there watching us swim and splash each other in the water. It was great fun. He thought it was very daring of Tricia and me to throw off our little hats that protected us from the sun. Women of the day didn't want a sunburn or a tan. I took down my hair and so did Tricia. It was another daring move. He listened to our brothers' objections, which we ignored.

Finally I couldn't take the badgering. "Ethan, Kurt, stop trying to parent us. We have made up our minds to ignore your suggestions. If you keep this up we are removing our swimming slippers too."

"Yes, it's not like you haven't seen our legs before." Tricia threatened.

Kurt laughed. "Ethan, let's not make this worse. They are declaring their independence."

"I wouldn't fight with them gentlemen. Once Lacey makes up her mind there is no changing it." Joseph Carlyle said as he came down the side steps and on to the sand.

"Hello Joseph!" I waved to him from the water.

"Lacey, can I speak with you for a moment." He yelled to me.

I made my way out of the water toward him. Kurt tried to be a gentleman about the situation, but I could tell it bothered him.

Joseph offered me a towel, but I refused it.

"I'll be going right back into the water. There is no need to dry off." I told him as I approached.

"You look beautiful with your hair down. I like the outfit. Are you free tonight at seven o'clock?" He asked me.

"No, I'm sorry Joseph. I've already made plans for this evening." I apologized.

"Oh, well then, would you be free tomorrow evening at seven o'clock?" He asked me.

"Yes, tomorrow night I am free." I answered.

"May I pick you up at seven o'clock? My parents would like to invite you to a late supper meal with us." He said.

"Just me?" I asked him.

"Yes Lacey, just you." He smiled.

"Alright. Tomorrow evening is fine. I'll be ready at seven." I told him. "Would you excuse me? I have more of the water and the sunshine to enjoy."

"Certainly. You have a fine afternoon." He turned and left us.

Kurt approached me after I was back in the water. "Lacey, what plans do you have tonight?"

"Just plans not to be taken for granted with last minute invitations." I replied and then I attempted to swim away from him.

He was too good in the water to let that happen. I continued to swim with him at my side. Then we stood up and let the water rush by us as we talked.

"Do you think the island is safe?" I asked him.

"The people seem to be very friendly. I didn't get a sense of danger, but I would not want Tricia or you walking the streets alone." He answered.

"What about Mr. Sheffield? What do you think of him?" I asked him.

"He has been very nice to all of us. He seems to be genuine." Kurt said. "Your face is a little red. You might want to put that swim bonnet back on."

"I think I will go back to my room and lie down. All this fresh air and water has made me very tired." I admitted.

"Alright. We'll see you later." He went back to swimming as I made my way back to shore and grabbed a towel.

I dried myself off as much as possible and went up to my room to change and take a nap. When I woke up I looked out the window and didn't see any of my companions on the beach. The house was quiet. I had no idea where anyone had gone. I decided to make my way to the grand room that had a piano in it. I sat down on the bench and started to play. I enjoyed playing the piano. It was relaxing. I didn't notice Mr. Sheffield enter the room. He surprised me by standing next to the piano.

"You play quite well Miss Lacey." He said.

"Do you play too?" I asked him.

"My wife loved the piano. We used to play duets and sing together." He said.

"You must do that with me. Do you have sheet music for it?" I asked him.

He smiled. "Yes, I do."

"Please, join me." I invited him to share the bench.

"Only if you call me Prentice." He said.

"Are you sure you want to allow me that privilege?" I asked him.

"I never sing a duet with a lady unless she continues to call me by my first name." He said.

"Very well then. Would you join me Prentice?" I smiled as I moved to the side to give him room to sit down.

He sat beside me and put the sheet music up. "Do you know this particular tune?" He asked me.

I looked it over. "It is a beautiful song. I know it well."

"You take the first note and I'll join in." He told me as he placed his hands on the keys.

I put my hands down to start my part and then we began. He had a beautiful deep voice that complimented mine. We sang the song all the way through without error.

"Mr. Sheffield, I am impressed." I declared.

"Prentice, Miss Lacey." He insisted. "You have a beautiful voice."

"Thank you. Shall we do this again? I enjoyed the experience so much." I told him.

"Let's." He removed the sheet music and put up another selection. "Whenever you are ready."

I started the first note and then we joined our talents on the piano. It sounded wonderful and relaxing. As soon as we finished with one song we went on to another. Prentice told me stories about his wife between songs. She sounded like a special kind of lady. He spoke with such love in his voice when he referred to her.

"You must have loved her deeply." I remarked.

"It is rare to find someone of the heart in this lifetime. She honored me by her behavior. I valued that about her. Even when we argued and that wasn't often, she was careful about what she said. She never called me names or belittled me. She would always make the case that I was a man of integrity and purpose. She made me want to be that man. She was a very positive person. If she had something derogatory to say, she would take the time to rephrase it so that I understood the point she was making, but without the negativity. She was very kind and supportive. I have missed her."

He captured my attention with his explanation. He was a very sweet man and that made him attractive. I thought my Aunt Mae would be quite taken with him.

"Prentice, have you ventured to find another woman to marry?" I asked him.

He laughed. "You have a boldness about you."

"I didn't mean to pry. I'm sorry if I did. You don't have to answer me. It is really none of my business." I apologized.

"Calm yourself Miss Lacey. I like your boldness. It is refreshing. Too many people skirt around the issues at hand and never get around to asking the questions they really want to ask. Please be as bold as you like. I enjoy it." He said.

I smiled. "Very well then. Prentice, has there been a lady on the island that might have captured your heart?"

"Several." He smiled. "The problem is that I am a Christian man and I have set myself a standard not to marry a gossip, or a complainer. Certainly, I seek a woman who loves Jesus. I need a woman who will pray for me. My wife was a prayer warrior. She had great faith in God's ability to love her completely and move each mountain she spoke to."

"I don't understand speaking to mountains." I questioned him.

"Jesus said certain specific things in the bible. If you go to the gospel of Mark, in the eleventh chapter at the twenty-third verse." He got up from his seat and sought out his bible. He turned to the page. "It says; *For assuredly, I say to you, whoever says to this mountain, 'Be removed and be cast into the sea,' and does not doubt in his heart, but believes that those things he says will be done, he will have whatever he says.* My wife believed Jesus meant that one hundred percent and that is how she prayed. Her prayers got results. She was careful to forgive those who had offended her so that unforgiveness would not get in the way of her prayers. She just believed she received it and it was hers. I am telling you that God moved the mountain for her. I need a woman who understands the power of God's declarations in this book. I have yet to meet one. Some think that God's word functions according to how good or bad they have been, but that is not true. God backs up his word because he cannot lie. If there is a requirement he spells it out. It is not a guessing game. This entire bible points to Jesus. He is always the focus. We will never be good enough, but we don't have to be, because God operates through us and he is always good enough. It is his virtue that heals. All he needs is for us to believe him. Jesus is the walking word of God. Just find out what is available to you in this book and speak it out and let Jesus walk it through to perfection. He is just looking for a vessel. My wife humbly knew she was not perfect, but God was. She just submitted herself as a vessel." He explained.

"How did you know that she was the one for you?' I asked him.

"She kissed me with her heart." He answered.

"I haven't kissed anyone yet. I'm not sure what you mean." I told him.

"You will know the difference when it happens." He assured me.

"You are an extraordinary man, Prentice." I was in awe of his love for God and his wife.

"I'm not extraordinary, I am just blessed." He smiled. "This time has been a delight to my heart Miss Lacey. I would enjoy doing it with you again in the future."

"Thank you Prentice. Do you know where the others have gone?" I asked him.

"Shopping." He answered. "I realized all of you have very

little provision of clothing. I sent them into town to shop. I had to get past Kurt and Ethan's pride so I offered them a job to work off some of the expense. They will start work tomorrow morning."

"What can Tricia and I do for you? You've been so kind." I offered.

"I will look into it, but I do not want you or Tricia rushing to work. Men should take care of women more often. Take a week to relax and then you two can join me in my inquiries about helping out somewhere as a volunteer. I don't want you to be at the mercy of a boss. You are much too precious to me as a friend." He said.

"You overwhelm me." I admitted.

"It is you Miss Lacey who overwhelms me. I am beginning to adore you and Miss Tricia." He said as he left me.

I continued to play the piano until Ethan returned with the others. I didn't hear them until they entered the room I was in.

"Lacey, I had no idea you could play the piano so well." Tricia remarked as she approached me. "The melody is beautiful. Please keep playing."

"Maybe another time. I have been at this for some time. I think I would prefer to find out about what you were doing." I told her.

She held up the packages toward me. "I felt an urgency to buy you some items when I was shopping. Mr. Sheffield has been most generous. I am anxious to thank him. Do you know where he is?"

I stood up. "I believe he went into the library, but I did hear someone else come into the manor. He might be meeting with that person. I only heard the butler greet him. I don't know who it is."

"We shouldn't disturb him." Kurt said. "Let's bring these things up to our rooms and thank him when we get a chance to see him."

"Did you enjoy the shopping?" I asked them.

"Yes. The people we met were very nice. The island has many things to choose from. I believe we will look quite dashing in some of these outfits." Ethan remarked as he reached his room. "I'll check in with all of you later."

Kurt was the next one to go into his room. Tricia and I brought the packages into Tricia's room. We opened them on her bed.

"Lacey, try on the things that appeal to you. I believe we are the same size. I bought ten dresses. Please choose the ones you like. I like them all, so to part with any is no sacrifice." She told me. "I also gathered some undergarments for us when I was able to avoid the watchful eyes."

"You have wonderful taste. I appreciate this Tricia." I told her.

"I enjoyed the adventure." She smiled. "I also picked out a very nice brush and comb for you, and some perfume. I hope you like it." She handed the small bottle to me.

I opened it and smelled it. "It's wonderful!"

"I know. I've never smelled anything so appealing." Tricia agreed. Then she went on to tell me about the shops and the people they met.

Once I settled on the five dresses I preferred, I carried them to my room, along with the other accessories.

We were all able to thank Prentice at the supper meal. After we ate he asked Ethan and Kurt to join him in the library. They politely excused themselves from us. They went into the library and Tricia and I took a walk around the property. The sun was still shining in the sky, so we had no worries as we strolled along.

"Gentlemen, I would like you to tell me more about your skills so that I can place you specifically where you are needed."

"I know about carpentry Sir. I can build a box or a house. The only thing I have not worked on is a ship." Ethan told him.

"And you Kurt?" He asked.

"I have lots of skills. Most recently I've worked as a fisherman. I know all aspects of operating a ship. I've loaded supplies, been at the helm, climbed to the crow's nest, done soundings, trimmed the sails and I was a Captain's assistant for a while. I've been a carpenter too. I'm sure that wherever you need me, I will be an asset to you." Kurt replied.

"Take two of the horses from my stable and use them to get to work tomorrow. You need to go to the harbor and ask for Mr. Jeremiah Banks. Ethan and Kurt you will be working on the ship I am currently building. I will send you with a letter of introduction. Mr. Banks will direct you to your assignments." Mr. Sheffield told them.

"We appreciate this opportunity Mr. Sheffield." Kurt said.

"Yes Sir, you've been so generous to us. Thank you." Ethan said.

"Just do your best. Be a team player. Helping others helps me." Mr. Sheffield replied.

"Mr. Sheffield, we don't want to take advantage of your generous hospitality for too long. Kurt and I plan on looking for a home for ourselves and our sisters as soon as we can afford it." Ethan told him.

"Gentlemen, I completely understand, but I must insist that you stay here another thirty days before you move." He said.

"Why is that?" Kurt asked.

"In order to obtain housing on the island you must have a sponsor who has known you for more than thirty days. Without that, even with money, you cannot be rented a place to live. It is the law. It prevents outsiders and criminals from settling here." He explained.

"That is a very stringent law." Kurt remarked.

"It was necessary to keep the people of the island safe and ensure that only the types of businesses that would compliment the island would develop here." He explained.

"Was the law in place when you and your wife moved here?" Ethan asked.

"No. It became necessary for those of influence on the island to pursue the establishment of the law after it was clear that this island was in danger of being taken over by pirates and criminals. It took us a few years to get rid of the criminal element, but once they were out, this law has kept them out." Mr. Sheffield explained.

"We appreciate your generosity in allowing us to stay with you the required number of days." Kurt said.

"You're welcome. It is truly a pleasure having you all here. I regret that I could not push you to stay longer. If you decide you would like to, there is no rush for you to leave. I do like the joy you all bring to this manor." Mr. Sheffield said.

Chapter Four

The next evening Joseph Carlyle came for me to transport me in his carriage to his parents' home. They had a beautiful estate. I was impressed with the size and elegance of it. Joseph explained that his mother was responsible for the décor as we walked through the hall on our way to the dining room.

His mother and father stood to greet me.

"Thank you for inviting me, Mr. and Mrs. Carlyle." I said politely.

"We really did want to get to know the girl that our son is so smitten with." Mrs. Carlyle replied. "Please make yourself comfortable Lacey."

Joseph pulled out my seat for me and helped me to sit. Then he sat next to me as his parents made themselves comfortable at the dining room table.

"Your home is so elegant Mrs. Carlyle. Everything is so beautiful." I commented.

"Thank you Lacey. I love to decorate. My husband moans each time I decide to change a room." She said.

"It is true. I just seem to get used to it and then she is

moving furniture and having new curtains designed." He told us.

The servants brought in the food and served the drinks to us as our glasses needed filling. I covered my glass as one of them attempted to pour the wine.

"No thank you." I smiled.

"Don't you like wine dear?" Mrs. Carlyle asked me.

"I've never had it. I prefer water or tea." I smiled.

"Never? That is surprising." Mrs. Carlyle remarked as she picked up her glass of wine.

I watched her sip it as Mr. Carlyle asked, "Can we convince you to try a sip of it Lacey? You may find it has a pleasant taste."

"I'm sure it is pleasant or you would not have offered it to me. Maybe some other time." I said graciously.

"As you wish." Mr. Carlyle replied.

"How has your stay been with Mr. Sheffield?" Joseph asked me.

"He is a delightful man. He plays the piano quite well and he has a beautiful singing voice. He has been very kind to all of us." I told them.

"Did he tell you how his wife died?" Mrs. Carlyle asked.

"I have never inquired and he has never offered the information. I'm not sure he wants me to know and if that were true, I would prefer to honor his privacy." I told her.

Joseph smiled at me and changed the subject. He knew that I had offended his mother by cutting off any tinge of gossip she wanted to indulge us in.

Mrs. Carlyle wanted more information about our lives. "I was shopping today and I saw your brother with the Stamos family. It seems they had a very blessed day shopping."

"You should have said hello to them. I am sure they would have appreciated it." I told her.

"I was in a hurry at the time or I would have." She replied. "I didn't see you among them. Were you off by yourself shopping?"

"No, I was resting at the manor." I replied.

"They left you at Mr. Sheffield's alone?" Her tone offended me.

"Is there a reason that would seem strange to you Mrs. Carlyle?" I asked her pleasantly.

"Juliet." Mr. Carlyle cautioned her.

"It was just a question Benjamin. I didn't mean anything by it." She replied to her husband.

Dinner conversation was a bit strained after that. Joseph found a reason to take me outside after we ate.

"I apologize for my mother. It seems she never understood why you turned down my proposal of marriage. I didn't realize until tonight that she had some bitterness in her heart about it. I am sorry Lacey. You didn't deserve that." He said sincerely.

"Your father was very gallant in saving me from defending myself to your mother." I told him.

"I would have defended you if she had continued. I was completely caught off guard by her comments." He said. "I will take up a conversation with her this evening. You will not be treated like that after tonight. I promise you."

"This evening did not go as I had expected. Your mother was very nice to me at the Sheffield house. I feel very uncomfortable being here Joseph. I know it is not your fault, but I would prefer that you take me home now." I told him.

Mrs. Carlyle overheard our conversation. She was quick to make her presence known. "Lacey, may I talk to you?" She approached me politely.

Joseph reached to my side and held my hand, showing his support of my decision.

"Of course." I answered as I looked down at our hands.

"I wish to apologize to you for making you feel uncomfortable tonight. I'm afraid my tone and my questions were inappropriate. I do apologize. I want you to feel welcome here. Joseph wants you to feel welcome here. Please allow me another chance to be the gracious hostess I should have been tonight." She waited for my reply.

"Maybe we were all a little nervous about tonight. Certainly I would like the opportunity to correct any misunderstanding that we had. I appreciate your kind words

Mrs. Carlyle." I told her.

"My husband and I are organizing a social gathering at the end of the month. We have arranged for musicians and for exorbitant amounts of food. Please let your family and friends know that we will be extending an invitation to them to attend, along with Mr. Sheffield. I would like to invite you personally. Please consider coming." She said.

"I would be delighted to attend and I am sure my brother and my friends would love to attend also." I smiled at her.

"Very good. Thank you Lacey. Excuse me please, my husband needs my company." She turned and left us.

I pulled Joseph's hand to my lips and kissed the back of it. "Thank you."

"I did nothing." He was surprised and smiled at me.

"Your gesture showed your mother and me the support you had for me. I appreciate it." I told him.

"I do love you Lacey." He declared softly.

"I wish I could say the same to you, but I cannot. We haven't known each other very long at all and I still intend to go on to America with Ethan. You should go back to England and find a girl who will appreciate you more." I told him.

"If I were to promise to go to America with you, would you give us more of a chance?" He asked me.

"Joseph, your life is with your family and they are here. Your aunts and uncles are in England. America has nothing to offer you." I told him.

"Lacey, it will take months for your brother to save up enough money to go on to America, and even much longer to pay for both of you to go. In that time you may both find that you like the island and don't want to move on to a place that has little to offer you. Please just give me a chance to affect your heart. With a sincere effort on your part I would be satisfied no matter what the outcome." He tried his best to convince me.

"Alright Joseph, I will give us a chance but there are conditions." I told him.

"What are they?" He asked.

"First, you should know that you are not the only man who has offered his affections to me." I told him.

"Who else?" He was very upset.

"You don't own me Joseph. We are not engaged or married and your attitude suggests that you view me as a possession. I am here to tell you that I will not be dictated to or pressured into a relationship." I stood my ground.

"For a very sweet girl, you certainly put me in my place." He decided to calm down. "Who is he?"

"I am sure I don't want to tell you right now." I replied.

"I seem to be stumbling over you tonight. First dinner and now my possessive attitude. Lacey, I apologize. I think you were right. I should take you home before I ruin this evening entirely. I promise that the next time you agree to my invitation, I will make sure that the evening has no pit falls."

"That sounds like a very good idea." I agreed.

He arranged for a carriage and took me back to the manor. He walked me to the door and said goodnight. I was walking up the staircase when Kurt came out of his room.

"How did your evening go?" He asked.

"Not as well as I would have expected." I told him.

He smiled. "Come tell me about it on the balcony. It's early."

"I should go to bed and call it a night." I said as I continued up the stairs.

He walked down and took my hand. He smiled at me. "Lacey, let's just talk. There is no harm in talking and it is so pleasant outside. The moon is full and the waves are crashing against the shore. You know you don't want to go to a lonely room. Please talk to me on the balcony."

"Alright." I turned around and we walked to the balcony together and leaned against the stone wall so that we could watch the waves rolling up to the shoreline in the moonlight.

"Breathtaking, isn't it?" I remarked to him.

"Yes it is. I've always loved that sound." Kurt said. "What happened tonight?"

"The good news is that the meal was incredible and the house the Carlyle family owns is beautiful and elegant." I told him.

"And the bad news?" He asked.

"I hate gossip, rumors and innuendo." I told him.

"Do you need a hug?" He asked.

"Actually, yes." I admitted.

He wrapped his big strong arms around me gently and held me close.

"You have the most incredible heart beat." I told him.

He almost laughed. "I do?"

"Yes. It is strong and steady like you. The sound of it makes me feel safe." I told him as I put my arms around him to hug him too.

"Lacey, what is going on that you are so unsettled about?" He asked me as he continued to hold me.

"Joseph asked me to give him a chance and I said yes." I admitted. I expected him to let go of me, but he didn't.

"And that makes you feel unsettled?" He asked.

"Yes." I answered.

"Why?"

"I didn't tell him your name, but I did tell him that you wanted the same thing." I told him.

"Continue." He wasn't demanding when he said it. I realized the unselfish confidence he possessed.

"The information upset him. He didn't like the idea that another man was interested in me. He demanded your name and I wouldn't give it to him. I told him that he didn't own me." I explained. "Kurt, do you have an opinion about that?"

"About his attitude or about the fact that two men are interested in you?" He asked.

I looked up at him as he continued to hold me. "About his attitude."

Kurt turned his head slightly and moved toward my lips with his. Every moment slowed down as I felt his breath seconds before he offered his lips to mine. He waited for me as if he were gently inviting me to kiss him. It was an incredibly romantic gesture and I welcomed it with my response. He left me breathless. Then he said softly and slowly, "Lacey, you are a very smart and beautiful lady. I don't have to explain my opinion about his attitude. Just follow your heart."

I moved gently out of his embrace and backed away from him. "I think I'd better go to my room."

He just looked at me with those incredible adoring eyes. Then he asked. "Are you sure you want to leave me now?"

I nodded yes.

"Goodnight Lacey." He smiled.

"Goodnight." I whispered and I left. When I was back inside the manor I ran up to my room.

"You made an impression." Mr. Sheffield said as he came out onto the balcony.

"Were you watching us?" Kurt asked.

"I happened to pass by just before you kissed her. I apologize for my invasion into your privacy. Do you love her?" He asked Kurt.

"I care about her. I'm attracted to her." Kurt replied.

"Did you know that unless she kissed Joseph tonight, which is doubtful, that is the first kiss Lacey has ever shared with a man?" Mr. Sheffield wanted him to know.

"How do you know that?" Kurt was surprised by what he said.

"I doubt she kissed Joseph because she was too upset when she came back from their evening together." He answered.

"No, not that. How do you know it was her first kiss?" He asked.

"She told me while you were out shopping that she had never kissed anyone. We were talking about my wife and it just came up. Please keep it to yourself. I don't want her to be embarrassed by it. I just wanted you to know that Lacey believes something special happened tonight. Don't play with her affections." Mr. Sheffield warned him and then he walked away.

"Wow." Kurt said to himself after Mr. Sheffield left the balcony.

Chapter Five

Joseph wanted me to be his personal guest at the ball, but I refused him. I explained that I wanted to be available to my friends and Mr. Sheffield. He was disappointed with my decision but made very little fuss about it.

Mr. Sheffield arranged for our transportation to Mr. Carlyle's home. The five of us walked in together. There were at least seventy people mingling at the ball. Mr. Sheffield introduced us to some of the people we hadn't met yet. The music started and the guests lined up to dance. Ethan asked Tricia. Mr. Sheffield saw Joseph heading my way and he invited me to be his dance partner before Joseph had a chance to reach us.

I smiled. "I would be delighted Prentice."

Kurt was surprised I called Mr. Sheffield by his first name. He watched as I took the arm of my escort and went on to the dance floor to join the others. Prentice lined up with all the men and I lined up with all the women. We bowed to each other as the music began. It was great fun to be able to dance again. I hadn't experienced such pleasure since we had left England.

"She is quite beautiful." Joseph remarked to Kurt.

"I agree. Lacey is quite beautiful as are the many other young ladies at this ball." Kurt remarked.

"Are you interested in Lacey?" Joseph asked him.

"Why do you ask?" Kurt continued to look out over the crowd as he asked the question.

"I love Lacey. I am pursuing a relationship with her." Joseph told him.

"How does Lacey feel about this?" Kurt asked him.

"She is giving us a chance. I have the means to pamper her and I intend to do that." Joseph told him.

Kurt turned toward Joseph and looked directly at him. "Lacey is a wonderful person. She has great character. I trust that in spite of all the niceties you might be able to shower her with, she will choose the man she trusts and loves. This is not about things, this is about character Joseph. On that I have you beat. Excuse me." Kurt walked away from him.

Joseph made his way to me after the dance. "Lacey, may I have the next dance?" He asked.

I smiled. "Yes, of course."

"Thank you for the dance, Miss Lacey. Please excuse me." Mr. Sheffield said as he bowed to me.

"It was a pleasure Prentice." I smiled as he left.

The music started and Joseph and I paired up as partners and danced with the others. He insisted on the next three dances. I looked around occasionally and saw Kurt mingling in the crowd. I was concerned that he had not approached me for a dance. After the fourth dance with Joseph, I excused myself and joined my brother and Tricia.

"Are you having fun Lacey?" Tricia asked.

"This reminds me of England." I told her.

"Yes it does." Ethan agreed.

"Some of the ladies seem to be flocking to my brother." Tricia noticed.

"He seems to be enjoying the attention." I remarked.

"I'm not sure. Kurt loves to dance and he hasn't asked anyone yet. It is so strange. He has never been shy." Tricia said.

"Excuse me please."

I made my way toward him and saw that he noticed. I saw him smile at me. Then Joseph intercepted my journey.

"Are you thirsty Lacey?" Joseph asked as he held out a glass of wine to me.

"Miss Lacey doesn't care for wine." Kurt said as he approached us. Then Kurt handed me a glass of water.

I smiled. "Thank you Kurt."

"You're quite welcome. Could I share the next dance with you Miss Lacey?" Kurt asked.

"I would love that." I answered before I took another sip of water from my glass.

The music started for a waltz. That irritated Joseph even more because the other dances had been partner dances among many people. This waltz would be more intimate.

"I requested this for us." Kurt informed me as he put his hand around me to touch me on my back.

I put my hand in his hand and put my other hand on his shoulder as the music started. "Why did you request a waltz?"

"I missed you and I didn't want to share you with anyone else during our dance." He confessed as he guided me on the dance floor.

"I saw you talking with Joseph earlier. Was he being nice?" I asked.

"He remarked how beautiful you looked and I agreed." He said.

"Is that all?" I asked him.

He leaned toward me and whispered in my ear. "Lacey, I don't want to share you right now and talking about Joseph seems like I am sharing you with him. Let's stop doing that. I missed you. I've talked to so many people tonight and it was difficult concentrating on their trivial conversations. All the time I thought of you and how you would feel in my arms when we danced. You are a complete distraction for me." He straightened up and smiled at me.

The rest of the crowd seemed to disappear as I looked into his eyes. "What happens after this dance?" I asked him.

"Predictably other men will approach you because of your

beauty and availability. I want you to enjoy yourself Lacey. I'm not worried about you with other men. I trust who you are. If they play another waltz please promise it to me. I will not be far away when the music starts." He said.

"May I promise you every waltz tonight?" I asked him.

"That is more generous than I expected, but I would be honored." He smiled. "You won't have to look for me. I promise I will find you."

"Thank you for the dance." I said to him as the music ended.

"It will continue to be my pleasure Miss Lacey." He bowed and backed away as Joseph approached me.

"May I have the pleasure of the next dance?" He asked me.

"Certainly Joseph." I smiled.

During the evening I danced with Prentice again, and Joseph, but I made sure that each time the musicians played a waltz I was dancing with Kurt. Each time he was a perfect gentleman, making himself available upon the first note and leaving me politely to enjoy the attention of others when the music ended.

After the third waltz Joseph approached me. "Have you reserved these dances for Kurt Stamos?"

"At the first waltz I offered to reserve each one for him. He has been very much a gentleman this evening. Are you upset about our arrangement?" I asked him.

"Yes Lacey, I am." He admitted.

"Why?" I asked him.

"A waltz is a very private dance shared by two people. The other dances are among many. He has found a way to have your undivided attention and I have not." He complained.

"You wear me down with your attitude of unfairness. I have danced the majority of the evening with you alone. Prentice has only shared three dances with me as has Kurt. I think your attitude is childish Joseph." I told him.

"You're absolutely right. I apologize Lacey. It is a ball and we should just enjoy ourselves. I'm sure I have monopolized too much of your evening. You are certainly free to dance with whomever you wish. Excuse me please." He left me standing alone and turned his attention to another young lady.

Kurt approached me immediately. "Are you surprised?"

I looked at him and smiled. "Not really. He has always come across as a bit spoiled."

"Better to find out these things early in a relationship." Kurt remarked.

"It's been a very exciting and wonderful evening, but I am very tired. I think I'll let the others know I have decided to go back to the manor." I told him.

"Without you here, there is no reason for me to remain. I will escort you home." He offered.

"Thank you. I'll be a minute. Ethan is just across the room and Prentice is next to him. I will let them know our plans." I told him.

"No, we will let them know our plans. I want to make sure Tricia will be fine without me here." He took my hand and we walked through the crowd together.

Ethan promised to watch over Tricia. Mr. Sheffield made his driver available to us. We said goodnight and then we found Mr. and Mrs. Carlyle and thanked them for inviting us. Joseph was busy flirting with the other young ladies so I left without making him aware of it.

When we arrived at the manor Kurt escorted me to my bedroom door.

"Sleep well Lacey." He said as I opened my bedroom door.

"Thank you for escorting me home. I will see you in the morning." I told him.

"Yes you will." He turned and left me.

Ethan knocked on my door in the morning. "Lacey, are you ready for church?" He asked.

I cracked the door open. "Oh no I'm not. I'm sorry Ethan, I must have overslept. Tell the others to go on without me. I'll stay here and see you all after church."

"You may be alone Lacey. The servants will be in church. Are you sure you will be fine here alone?" He asked me.

"I'm sure I will be fine. Just go. It will take me a while to get dressed and fix my hair. I'll see you when you get back." I told him.

"Very well. If you decide to go anywhere please leave me a note in my room." Ethan requested.

"I will." I smiled. "Now go or you will make the others late."

He left. Everyone was surprised when I did not join them.

"She overslept. She will be staying home today." Ethan told them.

"I'm sure she will be fine. My butler is still watching over the house. I trust Milton to keep an eye on her." Prentice assured the others as Ethan climbed into the carriage.

I got up and got dressed. I took my time brushing out my hair. Then I got a hat and put it on. My plan was to walk along the beach and enjoy the morning. I let Milton know where I was going. The light breeze of the ocean increased to a formidable wind at times. I had to remove my hat and hold on to it to keep it from blowing away. The sand was going inside my shoes as I walked so I slipped them off along with my stockings and stuffed my stockings into the pocket of my dress. I was sure I would get back to the manor before anyone had returned from church. I picked up my dress a little so that I could walk barefoot in the water as I strolled along the beach. It was low tide so I could see the fullness of the rocks that jutted out from the beach in a few places. I had walked quite a distance and decided to turn around and head back to the manor when my hat blew out of my hand. I watched it as the wind carried it out onto the rocks. I viewed the situation. I really didn't want to lose that hat after Prentice had been so generous to give us the money to buy it. I put my shoes down on the sand and made my way onto the rocks. They were slippery. My hat was caught among them. I reached for it and slipped. My foot got caught between two rocks as I sprained my ankle. The pain was nearly unbearable. I tried to pull my foot free but each movement sent waves of intense pain through my foot. I sat on the rocks and cried. Then my hat blew into the ocean.

As Prentice and the others entered the manor Milton got his attention. "Mr. Sheffield, Miss Lacey has been gone a very long time. She told me she was just taking a walk on the beach. I watched her when she began her walk. She went to the left of the manor, toward the inlets. I'm concerned. She told me she wouldn't be long."

"Kurt and I will go look for her." Ethan said.

"I'll join you after I get my horse. Hurry, the tide is coming in. Check the shoreline. Make sure you check the inlets and the rocks. You go on ahead of me. We must find her soon." Mr. Sheffield was very worried.

Kurt and Ethan ran down to the beach toward the inlets. They were met by a few children.

"A lady needs help." The children told them. "Please come."

"Show us the way." They followed the running children.

They heard me screaming and saw two men near me.

"That's my brother and his friend. They are trying to help the lady." One of the children told them.

I was crying when Ethan and Kurt got near me.

Ethan got down in the water next to me. "Lacey, calm down. We are here to help."

"Her foot is stuck between the rocks. Each time we try to pull her free she screams." One of the men explained.

"Lacey, give me a minute." Kurt put his hands under the water. He felt the bottom of my leg and my foot as far as he could. "Ethan she is really wedged in there. We can't pull her free. We have to move the rock without trapping ourselves. You two find me some small rocks about the size of my hand. We won't be able to pick up the large rock that has her foot trapped, but we might be able to move it enough to wedge a few smaller rocks under it to lift it away from her foot."

"The tide is rising. It just covered my foot when I got trapped and now it is covering my waist. I have no way to stand up." I continued to cry.

"Lacey, please relax. We won't leave you." Ethan told me.

The men came back with four smaller rocks. "Will these help?"

"I think so. Be careful now and come to this side of me. Ethan you push the rock up away from her foot as these two men pull it. Give me time to place the rocks. Please don't trap my hands. If you must let go, warn me." Kurt said.

They all agreed. The two men pulled up on the rock and Ethan pushed it back. Kurt put the rocks underneath away from my foot.

"Hurry Kurt, this rock is heavy." Ethan told him.

"Lacey pull your foot out as soon as you feel that you have enough room. The rocks are placed. Lacey, can you pull your foot out?" Kurt asked.

I tried. "No."

Kurt felt my foot again. "We need two more rocks about the same size."

The young men ran to find two more rocks. They came back in a few minutes and handed them to Kurt. Just then Prentice showed up on his horse. He had one of the children hold the reins as he made his way to all of us.

"What is the problem?" He asked.

"Her foot is trapped. We should be able to free it soon. I need you to pull her foot out as soon as she has the room to move it." Kurt told Prentice.

Prentice got down on his knees next to me.

"Mr. Sheffield, give me your hands and I will guide you to the problem." Kurt told him.

Prentice gave Kurt his hands and he guided them to my foot.

"Hold her here and here so that her foot doesn't break when you pull her free." Kurt told him.

Prentice nodded. "I'm ready."

"Okay gentlemen lift on three. One, two, three." Kurt counted.

All of them worked together to free me from the rocks. I yelled in pain as Prentice lifted my foot out.

"She's free." Prentice told them. "Thank God!"

They warned Kurt and he pulled his hands out. Then they let go of the rock.

Kurt was the strongest one there. He picked me up in his arms and carried me carefully off the rocks and placed me on the beach away from the water.

"What are you doing?" Ethan pulled Kurt's hand away from my foot.

"Relax Ethan. I am checking to see if anything is broken before we move her again. She's in pain. I want to know why." He said.

"Are you a doctor?" Ethan asked.

"No, but I know about these things. You have no reason not to trust me. Let me help her." Kurt insisted.

"Ethan, let him help me." I was crying.

He let go of Kurt's hand.

"Lacey, I'm going to touch your foot and ankle and the bottom of your leg. You tell me if you feel pressure or pain." He went slowly as he continued to ask me questions. Then he tried to move my foot slowly.

I yelled twice.

"It's a bad sprain and I suspect some of the bones have

been bruised, but nothing is crushed and nothing is broken. Some of your pain comes from being pinned between the rocks. You shouldn't walk on that foot. The swelling is increasing. We have to get your foot up and try to keep it cool. The cold water kept the swelling down. You'll be soaking that foot in the ocean tomorrow." Kurt smiled. "Let's get her back to the manor."

"Put Lacey on my horse." Prentice suggested.

"Prentice, I can't ride your horse in this dress." I told him as I started to calm down from the experience.

"Then I will get on my horse and the boys can hand you up to me. You can ride side saddle and I will hold on to you." Prentice suggested. "I would let Ethan do it, but this horse is particular about who rides him. He likes me and the ladies. Even I don't understand it."

I smiled. "Thank you Prentice. I appreciate you being my escort on your horse."

"Sounds like a plan. Get on your horse Mr. Sheffield and Ethan and I will help her up." Kurt said.

"Please let me thank the young men who helped me." I requested.

Prentice called them over to us and shook their hands. "We could not have done this without you. Thank you for coming to the aid of my friend, Miss Lacey."

"We were happy to help." One of them replied.

"We hope you will be fine Miss Lacey." The other one

said.

"Thank you both. I appreciate everything you did to help me." I told them.

Kurt shook their hands and so did Ethan. They wanted to stay long enough to make sure I got on the horse safely. Prentice got on his horse and Kurt and Ethan helped me to sit in front of him. Prentice held on to me while Ethan walked on one side of the horse and Kurt walked on the other. They took me back to the manor. When we got back Kurt carried me into the house and up to my room. Ethan got Tricia to help me change out of my wet dress and into dry clothes. Then Kurt came into my room and set my foot on pillows to keep it elevated.

"You are getting way too familiar with that foot." I joked with him.

"Does it hurt?" He asked.

"Yes, the pain goes from throbbing pain to stabbing pain." I told him.

"Mr. Sheffield is sending someone for the doctor to see if there is anything he can give you for pain." Kurt told me as he covered my foot with a light blanket.

"Please remove the blanket. It just adds to the pain and really you've already touched my foot a number of times. It is not shy of you any longer." I told him.

"You have beautiful feet." He said.

"I have one beautiful foot and one obviously ugly and

injured foot." I replied. "Thank you for what you did today. I was so afraid I would drown out there among the rocks. It was stupid to chase my hat on to those rocks. I should have thought about the danger and considered it more than I did."

"I was going to ask you what happened that caused you to get trapped. Which hat was it that you lost?" He asked.

"The beautiful blue one. It blew away from my hand and on to the rocks. When my foot became trapped it just blew into the ocean. Some large fish has probably swallowed it by now." I told him. "Kurt, how did you know my foot wasn't broken?"

"No exposed bones for one thing, and if your ankle was broken you would have jumped when I put pressure on your ankle bone." He explained.

"But how is it that you know all that?" I asked him.

"Tricia and I have lots of relatives. Among them is Uncle Peter. He is a doctor. I earned extra money in my youth driving him around from house to house. He never liked horses. So I handled the horses and he let me observe him treating his patients. Sometimes he even let me stitch them up. I think he suspected I might become a doctor one day. I loved the sea more." He explained.

"You have so much talent." I was amazed.

"I've just met more talented people than most. I love to learn new things. You rest. The doctor will be here soon to give you something for the pain." He went to leave me.

"Kurt, do you play card games?" I asked him.

"Yes, some." He answered.

"Could you teach me? Ethan thinks it is vulgar for a woman to know how to play cards. Do you think it is vulgar?" I asked him.

I didn't understand why he left the room laughing without giving me an answer. He went downstairs and asked Mr. Sheffield if he had a few cigars and a couple of hats.

"Yes of course. Would you like a cigar, Kurt?"

"It's not necessarily for me. I need to explain something later to Lacey." He said.

"Alright. Follow me." He took Kurt into the library and opened a cigar box. He handed him two cigars. "Milton can show you where I keep my hats. Just return them when you are done using them."

"Thank you, Mr. Sheffield." Kurt said. Then he turned to leave the room and decided he had one more question. "Mr. Sheffield, may I ask you why you have decided to let Miss Lacey call you by your first name?"

"I believe when a man asks a question he deserves an honest answer. Miss Lacey and I played the piano together. We sang together and talked at length. She is precious to me. There is something about her that touches my heart. That is why I asked her to call me by my first name." He answered.

"Mr. Sheffield, are you romantically interested in Miss Lacey?" Kurt asked him.

"There we go with another question. Mr. Stamos, Miss

Lacey is not interested in an old man. If I entertained thoughts of her in that way, it would be a complete waste of my time. Her heart is already set on someone closer to her age." He answered.

"Did she tell you that?" Kurt asked.

"She didn't have to." Mr. Sheffield replied.

Milton entered the room. "Mr. Sheffield, the doctor is here."

"Show him up to Miss Lacey's room." Mr. Sheffield said.

"Thank you again Mr. Sheffield." Kurt left the room and went right to Tricia. "Tricia, go quickly up to Lacey's room. Stay with her while that doctor examines her. She shouldn't be left alone in a room with a man she doesn't know, even if he is a doctor. You insist on staying with her. Hurry."

Tricia ran up to my room and entered after knocking once.

"There is no reason for you to be here Miss. I am here for Miss Lacey." The doctor told her.

"I'm afraid I have been ordered to stay with Lacey while you examine her. I don't want to upset the powers that be, so I'm staying." Tricia said.

The doctor was a little irritated. "Very well then."

He approached the bed. "What seems to be the problem?"

"I hurt my foot. I was told it was a sprain." I told him.

The doctor started to examine my foot. He was squeezing it and moving it and causing me great discomfort. I started crying and yelled a few times. Tricia left the room quickly and called out for Kurt.

"He is hurting her." Tricia told him as he ran up the staircase.

Kurt came into my room as the doctor was manipulating my foot and making me scream. Kurt put his hand on the doctor's wrist. "Stop now!"

"I am examining her foot." The doctor insisted.

"I said stop!" Kurt insisted.

The doctor put my foot down as I continued to cry.

"You tell me what you want to know and I'll get the answers you need." Kurt told him.

"I prefer to examine my own patients." The doctor objected.

"Not like this you're not. Miss Lacey has been through quite a bit of pain today and we want to avoid making her suffer unnecessarily. Ask your questions, specifically to me. If I cannot answer them, then we will discuss what comes next." Kurt said sternly.

Each question the doctor asked, Kurt answered. The doctor was impressed with his knowledge.

"I suspect you didn't need my opinion. Mr. Stamos is correct. You have a bad sprain and bruising against the bones of your foot. I have something your friend can mix up for your pain. Stay off the foot for at least a week. Mr. Stamos come with me and I will talk you through preparing the medication for her pain." The doctor said. He took Kurt out into the hall and went over the details. "Check her foot in a week. If the swelling is nonexistent and she can walk on it without pain then she can go about her business, but if it starts to swell and there is still pain, keep her off her feet for another week. She shouldn't need the pain killer after three days."

"I'll take care of it." Kurt said.

"I'm sure you will." The doctor replied.

"Just a word of advice for the future Doctor; talk to your patients first. It is a good way to avoid unnecessary pain." Kurt told him.

"Goodnight Mr. Stamos." The doctor left.

Kurt went down into the kitchen and mixed the medicine as he had been instructed. Then he brought it back to me in a glass. "Sip this Lacey. I'll tell you when to stop. I want to make sure it isn't too strong for you."

Tricia stayed with me. Kurt watched me for ten minutes.

"Lacey, how do you feel?" He asked me.

"A little tired and light headed." I told him.

"How is the pain in your foot now?" He asked.

"Not so bad." I told him.

"We are going to wait another ten minutes before you take any more of this." He said.

I was asleep in ten minutes. He covered me up and left me alone in my room.

"That pain killer is too strong for her. That doctor is dangerous. He told me to give her all of it at once. I've never met someone so incompetent." Kurt complained to Tricia.

"You have to tell Mr. Sheffield." Tricia insisted.

"I will." Kurt went downstairs and emptied the rest of the glass outside. Then he went to Mr. Sheffield and explained everything that happened. He described the doctor to Mr. Sheffield.

"That wasn't the doctor. That was the doctor's assistant. That man is an idiot. Thank you Kurt for stepping in to protect Miss Lacey. I shall have a few words with both the doctor and his assistant." Mr. Sheffield was very angry. He left the house immediately. He found the doctor at his office and insisted on speaking with him and his assistant. "I can import a doctor to take your place in a week!" He threatened. "If I ever hear of you sending this idiot out on a house call again I will have you evicted from this island with him. He assaulted my house guest by nearly breaking her foot and he prescribed enough pain killer to bring down a horse. If we had followed his instructions a very precious young lady would be dead right now. Now you keep him close or don't keep him at all! The next time I send for you Doctor, you make sure it is you who shows up! Is that clear?"

"Yes Sir, Mr. Sheffield. I sincerely apologize." The doctor said as he wrote out the correct dosage for the pain medication. "This is the correct way to mix the powder with water. I am truly very sorry. I was in a hurry to service someone else and I wasn't paying attention to the call. My assistant left me before I could stop him. I didn't have the advantage of time to go after him and when he returned he left out those details you just made me aware of. He is truly too zealous to be in the position of an assistant and too ignorant to know how dangerous his actions are. You will not see him again in any capacity that includes me or my profession." Then he turned to his assistant and fired him.

Mr. Sheffield left the office and returned home. Tricia was walking by the front door when he entered.

"Miss Tricia, how is Miss Lacey doing?" He asked.

"I just checked on her. She is still sleeping and still breathing. I only say that because that is the way Kurt wants it reported to him." She replied.

"Your brother is a fine man. Please give him these correct instructions on how to mix the rest of Miss Lacey's medicine." Mr. Sheffield said.

"Yes he is a fine man." Tricia smiled. "You look a little stressed Mr. Sheffield."

"I am. I was very concerned about Miss Lacey today, and then to find out that we nearly lost her twice upset me beyond words." He explained as he walked with Tricia.

"What do you mean twice?" She asked.

"My wife died on the rocks. The accident with Miss Lacey was nearly identical to my wife's accident. The only difference was that we didn't find Laura until after the tide had come in. She was trapped and she drowned."

"Mr. Sheffield, I'm so sorry. This must have been horrible for you today. I didn't realize that Lacey was in that kind of danger on the rocks." She said.

"It is my fault. I should have warned all of you of the dangers." He was distraught. "I just couldn't bear to bring up the explanation of her death. I'm so very sorry that my own grief caused me to keep that information from you."

"Mr. Sheffield, I understand. Just concentrate on the fact that Lacey is fine. She is resting and she will be fine." Tricia tried to comfort him.

"If it were not for your brother today, things might have turned out badly. I do appreciate all of you." He said.

"We appreciate you, Mr. Sheffield. You've been more than kind to all of us. I don't know where we would be if you hadn't taken us in like you did. Please don't worry. Everyone is safe and more than comfortable. Believe me, all of us would understand your reasons for not discussing your wife. It was a private matter. You could not have foreseen that Lacey would go out on to the rocks to chase her hat. Please rest Mr. Sheffield. I hate to see you upset like this. It hurts my heart." Tricia told him.

"Thank you, Miss Tricia. I will take your advice and retire to my room for a while." He left her and went to his bedroom and locked the door. He sat in the rocking chair beside his bed and cried.

I woke up late that evening and needed help but I was sure everyone was asleep. I threw off the covers and tried to ease myself to stand on one foot. My head was spinning as I stood up and I fell hard on to the floor. The sound woke Tricia in the next room and she came in to see what had happened.

"What are you doing on the floor?" She tried to help me up.

"I was dizzy and I couldn't keep my balance." I was rubbing my foot. "I hurt myself again. I'm afraid I can't help you much." I told her. "I need to relieve myself. There is no way to get where I need to go without help."

"I guess we hadn't thought much about that. I'll get Ethan to help you." Tricia said.

"No need." Kurt was in the doorway.

I looked up at him and I was embarrassed.

"Tricia follow us. I can get her there, but you have to help her once she is inside." He was referring to the outhouse.

"Oh God, kill me now." I said out-loud.

He chuckled and picked me up in his arms. "It could be worse. You could be trying to help me get there."

"I'm sorry I'm so much trouble for you. You've been wonderful about this." I told him.

"I'm happy to help Lacey. Don't worry about it." He told me as he carried me down the stairs.

We had to walk through the back yard to reach our destination. He put me down at the door of the outhouse and Tricia helped me to hop inside and stayed with me. Fortunately it had been built as a type of luxury accommodation so that Tricia had room to be with me.

"This is awful." I whispered to her.

"It is just life Lacey. You would do the same thing for me." Tricia whispered in reply.

"A week of this is bad enough. What do I do tomorrow while Ethan and Kurt are working? How do I get down here? I can't possibly use the pee pot. There is no way to balance over it with my foot like this." I told her.

"We'll think of something." Tricia replied. She helped me gather myself together and then assisted me in hopping out of the outhouse.

Kurt picked me up again. "How is your foot?"

"I hurt it when I fell. It still hurts." I told him.

"Tricia, go back to bed. I'm going to take Lacey into the kitchen and mix up the pain medicine for her. I'll make sure she gets to bed." Kurt told her.

"It's late Tricia. You need your sleep. I'll be fine." I told her.

"Alright. Just call me if you need me. I can hear you through the wall." She told me.

We watched her walk ahead of us into the manor.

Kurt carried me into the kitchen and sat me on the kitchen counter. "It's easier to lift you off of there and it will keep your feet from touching the floor while I put this together." He went into the cabinet and grabbed the package of powder that had to be mixed with water. "This package looks different than the other one I mixed earlier." He tried to read the writing on it. "Isn't anything on this island marked clearly?" He measured out the powder with a spoon and put it into a glass. Then he added water to it and stirred it until it was blended. "Drink this." He handed me the glass.

"Kurt, will this put me to sleep again?" I asked him.

"Probably." He said.

"What if I only drink half of it?" I asked him.

"It might dull the pain, but it won't get rid of it." He said.

"I'll take my chances. I don't like being unconscious for the sake of my comfort." I told him.

"Drink it. It is late and you need your sleep. Drink half tomorrow." He suggested.

I took the glass and sipped it. "It's awful."

"Drink it fast." He told me.

"No, I will suffer through sipping it just so I can spend time awake with you." I said.

"I'm flattered, but I am tired too. I have to work in the morning." He said.

"You're right. I'm being selfish. I'm sorry for keeping you up." I tried to drink it fast, but I couldn't stand to do it all at once. I got about half of it down. "Just give me a moment."

"Alright." He smiled.

"I don't feel good." I put the glass down.

"What's wrong?" He was concerned for me.

"My head feels like it is heavy and my arms are disappearing. I can't feel them." My eyes rolled up in my head and I was unconscious.

Kurt grabbed the package again and the instructions from the doctor. He was sure he mixed it exactly as the doctor had written it out. He laid me on the counter and turned my head to the side. Then he ran to Mr. Sheffield's bedroom and banged on the door. "Mr. Sheffield get up! It's Lacey. I need your help!"

Mr. Sheffield came to the door and opened it. "What's wrong?"

"It is that damn medicine again. Come with me." They ran into the kitchen. "Help me to get her off the counter. We have to keep her walking. You have to send someone for the doctor."

"Milton! Milton!" Mr. Sheffield yelled.

Milton had a bedroom near the kitchen. He came out to see what was so urgent. "Wake up Ethan and Tricia and send Jamison to fetch the doctor. Tell him to throw him over his horse if he has to, but get him here. Hurry!"

Milton ran to bang on Ethan's door and Tricia's. He told them they were wanted in the kitchen. Then he ran outside to the stable and woke up Jamison. He sent him to get the doctor. The doctor arrived twenty minutes later.

"What happened?" He asked.

"I mixed that medicine according to your directions and she only drank half. She said her head felt heavy and her arms disappeared. Then her eyes rolled up in her head and she was out. We've been dragging her across the kitchen for twenty minutes to keep her heart beating. She is more aware, but in bad shape."

"Where is the package you mixed?" The doctor asked.

"On the counter." Kurt told him.

The doctor looked at it. "This isn't good. I thought he gave you something else. She has too much of this in her system. He told me he gave her something else. I'm so sorry. We have to get her to swallow this mixture." He mixed up something that looked black.

"Kurt?" Tricia asked for his opinion.

"He's right. That will help her, but she is going to fight it. Tricia leave us. You don't want to see this." Kurt told her.

"Lay her on the table." The doctor instructed. "You and you, hold her down." He said to Ethan and Prentice.

Kurt adjusted my head. He knew what was coming.

The doctor took a tube out of his bag.

"What is that for?" Ethan asked.

"He is going to put it into her mouth and then push it into her stomach. He has to pour the mixture into the tube. It is activated charcoal. It will bind to the poison in her body and save her life. If you can't bear to watch, turn away. Just hold her still. She will fight this." Kurt told him.

Ethan thought he could watch, but he couldn't. He held on to me and put his head down as he listened to me panic, fight and gag. The doctor finally pulled the tube out.

"Ethan." I was crying as they all let go of me.

He came to me and put his hand on my forehead. "It's alright Lacey."

"Please make them go away." I cried.

"Please leave us alone." Ethan asked them.

"I should stay." The doctor said.

"Lacey, can the doctor stay?" He asked me.

"Please make them leave the room. All of them." I continued to cry.

"Doctor, please leave us alone until I come to get you." Ethan said.

They all left.

I sat up on the table and put my arms around my brother's neck and cried on his shoulder. "Take me out of here."

"Where do you want to go?" He asked me.

"Outside. I want to be away from this room." I told him.

"Okay Lacey. I can take you out to the patio." He offered.

"No. Go move a chair next to the out-house. I fear I will

need to be near it. I don't feel well at all. I am humiliated from this experience. I feel well enough for the doctor to leave me. I won't be taking anything else for pain. I don't trust it. I will be happy to suffer through the discomfort. I don't want to see Mr. Sheffield or Kurt tonight. Please tell them and move me outside." I tried to stop crying.

"Do you want Tricia to help you?" He asked.

"Please." I answered.

"I'll ask Kurt to send her to us. Give me a minute." Ethan left me in the kitchen for a few minutes. He found the men waiting near the door of the kitchen. "Lacey would like some privacy. She wants all of you to leave us alone. I am taking her outside. She will be needing Tricia. Kurt, could you ask Tricia to join us in the back yard?"

"Certainly." He left immediately to get her.

"Doctor, you can check in on her tomorrow evening." Ethan told him.

"Very well. She seems better. I believe everything will pass out of her body. Please let me get that powder from the kitchen and replace it with what she should have for pain." The doctor said.

"Not until you and I have a talk." Mr. Sheffield said.

"Doctor, my sister will not take any more medicine for pain. Her trust for it is at an end, as is mine." Ethan told him.

"What about her discomfort?" The doctor asked.

"She is determined to endure it." Ethan answered.

The doctor was surprised. "If that is what she wishes to do. If she changes her mind we can discuss it tomorrow evening."

Tricia was dressed when she came downstairs. "Ethan, where is Lacey?"

"In the kitchen waiting for us. Goodnight Gentlemen." Ethan said.

Ethan opened the kitchen door and Tricia walked through it. He followed her. He picked me up from the table and carried me outside. We spent the evening near the outhouse. Tricia was a great comfort and help to me. She went into the house and got a few blankets for Ethan. She spread them out on the lawn and we watched him sleep. We only woke him up when we needed him. We watched the sun come up and then Tricia woke Ethan up so he could get ready for work. He promised to come back down to carry me upstairs before he left.

A few minutes later Kurt was in the back yard. He came to see me. "You girls look tired. How do you feel Lacey?"

"Better, thank you." I answered.

"May I carry you to your room?" He asked.

"It's not necessary. Ethan is coming back to us." I said.

"He is visibly tired Lacey. Please let me do this for you both." Kurt asked.

"I'm such a mess." I was embarrassed.

"You look beautiful to me. Please Lacey." He asked again.

"Alright. Thank you." I put my arms around his neck and he picked me up.

"I had the servants fill a bath for you when I woke up. I thought you might want to refresh yourself. I had them put one in Tricia's room too. There are two nice women in your room to help you in and out of the tub. If there is a problem Ethan won't be leaving with me for another thirty minutes. Just send for one of us." Kurt said as he carried me upstairs.

I smiled. "I don't think I'll be sending for you, Mr. Stamos."

"That was worth a smile. You girls enjoy your day. Mr. Sheffield arranged for Jamison to be available to you today. If you have to be carried anywhere, he will do it." Kurt told me.

Tricia went into her room to take a bath and rest. "I'll see you later, Lacey."

"Thank you Tricia." I told her as she went into her room.

Kurt carried me into my room and put me on the bed. "Lacey, this is Mindy and Emma. They will help you. I'll check on you when I get home."

"Have a good day Kurt. Thank you." I told him.

He smiled at me and left, closing the door on his way out.

"Mindy, please lock the door before we get started." I told her.

A few days later Joseph stopped by for a visit. He came up to my room and visited with me at the side of my bed. "I heard what happened to you on the rocks. I'm very grateful you got the help you needed in time. Mr. Sheffield's wife wasn't so fortunate when the same thing happened to her."

"I heard about that." I told him.

"I wanted to apologize to you Lacey for acting the way I did at the dance. I was being childish. It's just that I love you so much and it pains me that you have an attraction for Kurt Stamos." He explained.

"Joseph, you are quite a bit older than me. You are eight years older and I just don't think we are suited to each other. I seem to be upsetting you all the time. First in England and now again here. I just think you should look for someone who would appreciate you more." I told him.

"You promised to give me a chance. Are you breaking that promise?" He asked.

I was frustrated with his persistence. "I don't want to keep disappointing you. You are expecting my feelings to change toward you and I just don't see that as a possibility now."

"What happened between you and Kurt Stamos that cancelled any chance you were willing to give me?" He asked.

"Nothing really. Kurt and I are friends now. He is kind to me, that's all. I am in no condition to carry on with anyone as you can see by my injured foot. I am confined to this bed most of the time for the next week. Joseph, in this life people know what they want and what they don't want. I don't understand why you claim to love me. You haven't known me very long at all. I don't want to be responsible for hurting you over and over again. I know that I don't love you and that I won't love you in the future. There is just nothing for me to build on with you. I'm sorry." I apologized.

"Lacey, there is magic between us. I feel it every time I get close to you." He held my hand and looked at me intently. "I can't walk away from you until I have convinced you of the possibility of the love we can have for each other. You are beautiful to me. I adore you." He leaned over and forced a kiss on me. When I went to pull away from him he wouldn't stop.

"Mr. Carlyle!" Tricia yelled at him. "Leave now!"

Joseph was startled by Tricia. "Lacey, I'm sorry. I shouldn't have done that."

"No you shouldn't have. Don't come back Joseph. I don't ever want to see you again." I declared.

"Lacey please forgive me." He tried to apologize.

"Leave now Mr. Carlyle or I will scream for help." Tricia threatened him.

He turned and left the room and the manor.

Tricia came to me and hugged me. "I had no idea he was in here. I would have never let him be in here with you alone. Are you alright Lacey?"

I held on to her tightly. "Thank you so much for coming when you did. I didn't know how to get away from him. I can't believe he had the nerve to try something like that. What is wrong with him? Does he just believe he is entitled to treat me that way?"

"You should tell Mr. Sheffield about this." Tricia said as she let go of me.

"I'm ashamed Tricia. I can't tell him."

"It wasn't your fault Lacey. Someone let him into this house and let him into your room. I for one want to know who that was. Don't you?" Tricia asked.

We heard Ethan and Kurt coming upstairs.

"Tricia please don't tell them." I begged her.

"Sorry Lacey, but this is not a secret I can keep from Ethan or Kurt. They will hate me for it." She left the room and met them on the steps.

"Did you pass Joseph Carlyle on the way in?" She asked the two of them.

"Yes, he was leaving on his horse." Ethan replied. "Was he here to see Lacey?"

"He was here to force himself on her." Tricia declared.

"What are you talking about?" Ethan pushed past her as he asked the question and came directly to my room followed by Kurt.

I looked up at both of them and pulled the covers over my face and held them there. "Go away. I have been humiliated enough for one day."

Ethan came to the bed and pried the blankets off my face.

"Look at me. I want an explanation now."

"Joseph came to visit and spoke about loving me. I told him that I wasn't interested in him and I thought it was best if he found someone else who could appreciate him more. We were just talking. He wanted to convince me that I loved him so he kissed me." I explained.

"Lacey, tell them the truth!" Tricia demanded.

"The truth Lacey." Ethan demanded.

"Promise me that you will not go after him. I don't want you to complicate this with more trouble. It will just spiral out of control and something that isn't so big will become too enormous for us. Please promise me that you will keep whatever outrage you feel about this between us. Please Ethan. Please Kurt. Please promise me." I begged them.

Ethan turned to Tricia. "I'm not about to make that promise. You tell me what happened here."

"Tricia please don't." I begged her.

"He came up here alone to her room. I walked in on him forcing her to kiss him and she was fighting to get him away from her and he wouldn't stop until I yelled at him." Tricia blurted out.

I tried to grab Ethan's arm before he got off the side of my bed, but he was up and out of the room too quickly. "Ethan, please stop. Please."

Kurt went after him and stopped him on the staircase by grabbing his arm. "Ethan, stop a minute."

"For what? He deserves to be knocked into next week for what he did to my sister." Ethan insisted.

"And he expects that is just what will happen. He will be waiting for you. You will be at a disadvantage. You are at one already because you are angry." Kurt told him.

"Aren't you? Aren't you angry about this too? I know you care for Lacey. Come with me and we will destroy him together." Ethan said.

"Of course I'm angry. She had no way to get away from him and he knew it. He is not some simple man who acts impulsively. He calculates his moves. I've done my homework. I wanted to know what I was up against when I asked Lacey to give us a chance and she said Joseph was in the running too. You underestimate him; I won't. When he feels pain from me, it will be as unexpected as that kiss was to her. All I am asking is that you calm down and do what Lacey wants you to do for now. Don't give Joseph what he expects, give him what he doesn't expect." Kurt said.

"What do you propose?" Ethan asked.

"Come with me." Kurt escorted him in to see Mr. Sheffield. "Sir, Ethan and I have a problem and we need your help."

"Sure, sit down. Let's talk." Mr. Sheffield told them.

Kurt explained everything that happened. "What does the law of the island say that we can do to seek after justice?"

"Well you can't duel with guns or swords, but there is a well known challenge you can present to despicable Mr.

Carlyle, a fist fight of honor." Mr. Sheffield said.

"Can you set it up for me?" Kurt asked.

"No, you are not related to Lacey. I can set it up for me because she was my house guest or I can set it up for Ethan because he is her brother." Mr. Sheffield explained.

"That is fine with me. Set it up for me Mr. Sheffield." Ethan said.

"Are you sure you can beat him Ethan? Put your pride aside and be honest with yourself. I don't know the man, but if there is a chance you will lose it may cause Lacey more humiliation because the reason for the fight will have to be disclosed." He explained.

"I can beat him." Ethan said confidently.

"You should be aware of the rules. No weapons. Fifteen minutes from beginning to end and no one can stop this fight unless someone cheats. He could kill you and he won't be punished for it. Keep that in mind." Mr. Sheffield told him.

"Set it up." Ethan declared.

"Alright, I'll set it up." Mr. Sheffield told him. Then he left the house immediately and rode over to the Carlyle home.

Benjamin Carlyle answered the door. "Can I help you Prentice?"

"Yes, could you call your son down? We need to have a very serious conversation." Mr. Sheffield told him.

Benjamin yelled upstairs to Joseph and asked him to come

downstairs. Joseph joined them in the sitting room.

"Mr. Sheffield has an important matter to discuss with us." Benjamin told his son.

Joseph didn't say anything. He just listened.

"This afternoon you came to visit my house guest Lacey Dopolis. The report I received of that visit stated that you entered her room alone, unannounced, without a chaperone or an escort. Then you discussed your feelings of love for her and when she responded by asking you to move on with your life without her in it, you forced a kiss on her and you were unwilling to stop when she tried to fight you off." Mr. Sheffield stated.

"Joseph, is this true?" His father asked him.

"I am ashamed to say that it is all true." Joseph admitted.

"According to the law of the island a challenge of honor can be made on behalf of the injured party. Ethan Dopolis is conveying that challenge through me. At six o'clock this evening he will meet you on my property for a bare fisted fight in an effort to restore the honor of his sister. Do you accept that challenge?" Mr. Sheffield asked.

"And if I don't?" Joseph asked.

"Then you will be put into the stocks in the center of town for a day and face the scorn of the town. Which do you prefer?" Mr. Sheffield asked him.

"Is that true Father? The stocks?" He was surprised.

"Yes, it is true. You face Ethan with your fists or I turn you over to Elliot and he locks you in the stocks in the middle of town for a day, sunrise to sunset. You will be at the mercy of anyone who wants to assault you, including Ethan Dopolis." His father explained.

"Very well then. I want you to know that I have no desire to have this fight, but I will." Joseph agreed. "What are the rules to this challenge?"

"No weapons allowed. Fifteen minutes from beginning to end. Then you both walk away satisfied with the outcome and never visit the situation again." Mr. Sheffield said.

"What if I kill him in those fifteen minutes?" He asked.

"Then you kill him. The law is the law. No one stops it no matter what happens unless either party cheats." Mr. Sheffield explained.

"Tell Ethan I will be there at six." Joseph said.

"I want you to know Joseph, that if I were matched in age with you, I would have challenged you myself. What you did to dear, sweet Lacey was despicable and an insult to my home and me personally." Mr. Sheffield was angry.

"I am sorry beyond words, Mr. Sheffield, but I will not lie down and be beaten by Ethan Dopolis. My goal was to work out my apology with Lacey. This has certainly complicated that solution. My apologies to you Mr. Sheffield. Please forgive me. You can be sure my recent behavior toward Lacey will not be repeated." Joseph and his father watched as Mr. Sheffield left their home.

At six o'clock Joseph showed up with his father. They

went out to a section of the back yard with Mr. Sheffield, Kurt and Ethan. None of them knew that Tricia and I were watching from inside the house. Jamison had helped me down to the library after they went outside.

"Fifteen minutes gentlemen, on my count." Mr. Sheffield said as they removed their shirts, shoes and socks.

"I'm sorry about how I behaved toward your sister." Joseph apologized.

"I'm sure you will be." Ethan replied as he got close to Joseph.

"Gentlemen, begin now." Mr. Sheffield said.

Ethan hit Joseph immediately and sent him flying backward. Then the fight was on. It was a pretty even match, almost blow for blow. Every time Ethan got hit my heart hurt for him. I looked at Benjamin Carlyle's face and he didn't seem concerned at all. I didn't understand it until the last five minutes and then Joseph showed what he knew how to do. He had been holding back his skill. Tricia helped me to move closer to the library window and cranked it open when we knew Ethan was in real trouble. Joseph got Ethan in a choke hold. We all knew he was moments away from killing him.

Joseph yelled out to me. "Lacey! Is this what you wanted to happen? Was this your idea?"

"No. Please Joseph stop this." I yelled out the window.

"I'm sorry for what I did. I'm sorry it has come down to this. Will you forgive me?" He asked as he held on to my brother.

"Yes, but please let him go." I begged.

"Give me your word that you will give us another good chance to find love and I will stop this right now." He yelled.

"I give you my word." I said without hesitation and he let Ethan fall to the ground.

"Tricia, go to Ethan. Hurry!" I told her.

Mr. Sheffield waited one more minute and stopped the fight. Joseph walked away with his father, and Kurt helped Mr. Sheffield carry Ethan into the manor and up to his room.

I sat in the library crying while everyone rushed to help Ethan by tending to his bruises and wounds.

Ten minutes later Kurt came into the library. "Do you want to see your brother? We've cleaned up most of the blood. He is resting."

I was still crying when I said yes.

He picked me up and carried me to Ethan's room and helped me to sit on the chair next to his bed. I held his hand. His face was bruised and swollen and his neck had marks on it from Joseph's hands. His lips were bloody.

"I'm so sorry for all of this Ethan." I cried. "This is my fault. I'm so sorry."

"Stop that Lacey." He said. "This wasn't your fault."

I just continued to cry. I was heartbroken that my brother looked so bad.

"Lacey, it looks worse than it feels. I'll be fine. I'm sorry I failed you. I think we all underestimated him." Ethan squeezed my hand affectionately.

"Please let this be the end of it Ethan. Please." I begged him.

"The rules are the rules. We walk away satisfied that we did our best." Ethan said. "I can't bear to see you cry."

"I'll let you rest and let Tricia take care of you now." I continued to cry. "Kurt, please take me to my room."

He picked me up and carried me to my bed. He put me in it. "Lacey, I'm sorry. This is my fault. I thought I would be the one fighting Joseph. I didn't understand the rules until it was too late and there was no way to stop Ethan without insulting him."

"Please just keep checking on him." I sobbed.

"Lacey, you can't give Joseph another chance. You can't trust him." Kurt said.

"I can't do this anymore tonight. I just can't. My brother is beaten and broken. I'm stuck in this bed and destined to give a monster one more chance. You can lecture me all you want and nothing will change. I gave my word to save Ethan's life. You know Joseph would have killed him. I gave my word and I refuse to go back on it. Joseph Carlyle has won himself another chance. Please leave me." I continued to cry as he shut the door.

Chapter Six

A few weeks later I was up and walking around. My foot felt much better for short walks. Ethan and Kurt were working ten hours a day and five on Saturday.

Joseph sent word to me that I should expect him to pick me up on Saturday morning and take me out for the day. I knew the day would come, but I wasn't looking forward to it.

"Lacey, I'm worried about you." Tricia said.

"I'm worried about me too. Joseph wants this to work. He will continue to put his best foot forward until I tell him to go away. I am aware of his personality. I will make sure I am surrounded by protectors when I end this." I told her.

At ten o'clock Milton came to tell me that Joseph was waiting at the door for me. I walked down the stairs to greet him. He still had some fading bruises on his face.

"Hello Lacey. Are you ready to go?" He asked.

"Yes." I took his hand as he offered it and went outside.

He helped me into his carriage. Then he got in beside me and took the reins. "I know that you are probably nervous about this, but on my word I promise I will be an absolute gentleman. I am truly sorry for my part in your suffering and the suffering of your family."

"Thank you." I responded.

He guided the horses toward his parents' property and then out to an open meadow. "I had the servants look over this area to make sure we wouldn't be bothered by any creatures. It is safe." He said as he stopped the carriage.

He got out a blanket from the back of the carriage and a picnic basket. After he set it up he came back to the carriage to help me out. "I thought we could just talk to each other, like we used to do."

During the next two hours his manner was gentle and caring. He made a great effort to enjoy my company. We talked about his plans for the future. We talked about America and what that might hold for me. I remained cautious, but I made a sincere effort to keep my word and give us a chance.

"I think I've worn you out enough for today." Joseph said. "I should bring you back to the manor."

"You've been very kind today Joseph. I appreciate it." I told him.

"Lacey, I've learned my lesson. I understand that you are a woman who regards the character of a man more than the substance of his wallet. It took me all of what happened to realize that you have higher standards than most women. Truly Lacey, I want to be that kind of man for you. I know I forced you to give us another chance. I'm not proud of my tactics, but I was desperate. I am so completely in love with you that it hurts my soul when we are separated. Please let me show you that my desire to change will rule my actions. Let me see you again." He waited for my response.

"I gave you my word that I would give us a real chance. I will keep my word. You may call on me again Joseph. I want you to understand something though. My heart will follow its own direction. You cannot force its way. I cannot promise you that I will be able to love you. I don't want to hurt you Joseph. Truly that is not my intention." I told him.

"I understand. Please let your heart have the freedom to choose. Don't hold it back because of our past. That is all that I ask. Just keep it open to the possibility of us being together." He said. Then he helped me into the carriage. He collected the blanket and the basket and put them in the back. Then he climbed in beside me. "I had a wonderful time Lacey. I would like to see you again next Saturday morning. Is that alright with you?"

"Yes Joseph, that would be fine." I smiled.

Kurt and Ethan avoided me that evening. It seemed I was getting the silent treatment from both of them. I spent my evening talking to Prentice on the balcony after supper.

"Lacey, they just don't know what to do about this situation. Your brother doesn't want you hurt and he feels responsible for your current situation. Kurt has feelings for you and it is probably driving him crazy that Joseph is part of your life. They will calm down in time." He said.

"I feel like they hate me." My voice gave away my sorrow.

"Sweet Lacey, they don't hate you at all." He put his arm around me like a father would to comfort me.

"Joseph was genuinely nice to me today. He wasn't so full of himself. He seemed to change. He said he realized that he had been awful toward me and he was sorry. I believed he was sincere and I did promise to give him a real chance. I have to keep my word." I told him.

"It is a learning experience for all of us Lacey. I hope Joseph is this man you think he can be, but it has been my experience that a man will not change unless God changes him. Find out if he has a relationship with God. If he is doing all this on his own, as soon as you disappoint him things could become worse than they were before." Prentice warned me.

"Prentice, I hope you are not insulted by this, but I feel like I am with my father when I am with you. I feel safe and loved." I told him.

"I am honored that you consider me in that way. You Lacey are more like a daughter to me than a dear friend. You have touched my heart in very special ways." He said.

The next two days for me were very lonely. I missed conversations with Kurt and Ethan. Tricia told each of them they were being childish and she was frustrated with their silence toward me. Prentice stayed out of it and patiently waited for them to come to their senses.

I was sitting outside alone in the back after supper when Ethan came out to talk to me.

"Lacey, can we talk?" He sat next to me.

"I would really love that Ethan." I told him.

"I've been guilty of avoiding this conversation and hurting you in the process. I'm sorry." He apologized.

"If you will just continue to talk to me and not shut me out, I will forgive you anything. I've missed you Ethan." I told him.

"Lacey, I feel responsible for the situation you are in now. I knew I had to do something about Joseph, but my decision to do what I did must have been wrong because now you are forced to spend time with him. My own humiliation has made me very angry at you and that was unfair. You are not responsible for any of this. I know you were just trying to save my life. I'm sure he would have killed me if you had answered another way. For a time I wished he had. I would have kept my pride at the expense of my life. Now I realize how dangerous pride is. The only real payment it demands is stupidity." Ethan explained.

"Ethan, your life was worth any bargain, but truly Joseph has been very nice to me. He is sorry for causing so much pain and I believe him. Your greatest success in this was that you convinced him that he was wrong in his treatment of me. You did restore my honor by your sacrifice." I told him.

"Lacey, please be careful around Joseph."

"I am very cautious around him. He has not even attempted to hold my hand. I've given my word to him and I intend to keep it, but when I am sure there is no hope of love toward him I will end it. I've decided to give him this chance. We've only been out on one picnic and he was very kind and considerate. Please don't worry. I don't believe he will overstep again. He worries about losing me." I told him.

"I will continue to be concerned Lacey because I love you. I don't trust him. I will not shut you out again. I was foolish to put you through all this silence." He got up and kissed me on the cheek. "If you need me for anything I am here for you."

"Thank you Ethan. I know Tricia is waiting for you. Go now and be with her." I said.

He smiled and walked away.

Kurt avoided me during the week. He didn't speak to me at all. When Saturday morning came he watched as I walked to the front door to meet Joseph. He watched me take his hand and leave with him.

"You are not helping the situation Kurt." Tricia whispered to him as he turned to walk away.

"She is giving him a chance. I am just supporting her decision." Kurt replied.

"You are not supporting her at all. You have put her out there alone with no support. Do you think that she will run to you if he hurts her this time? Why would she? Your silence judges her every day. You stand waiting with an, *I told you so*, remark when pain comes her way. Lacey is a good person who is doing what she believes is right. Your disapproval of her decision is obvious. Would you rather she not be a person of her word? Would you have preferred that she let Joseph kill her very own brother? Stop lying to yourself Kurt. You love the girl and you are worried and jealous. That is why you are acting the fool." Tricia walked away and left him with those words.

Joseph took me for a walk on the beach. Then he took me back to his parents' house and had the servants make us lunch. We talked for a while. Then he asked me to walk around the property with him.

"Can I hold your hand Lacey?" He asked politely as we walked.

I put my hand in his and we continued to talk. We stopped for a minute at the edge of the property.

"Lacey, the last time I kissed you was awful for you. I don't want that memory to overshadow us and the only way to replace it is with another kiss. May I kiss you the right way this time?" He asked.

"I'm not ready for that yet." I told him.

"That's fine. I don't want you to do anything you don't want to do. I've learned my lesson." He smiled.

"Thank you Joseph. You've been very kind and considerate. I appreciate your patience." I said.

"Lacey, how are things between you and Kurt Stamos?" He asked.

"He hasn't spoken to me in days." I told him.

"It is truly his loss." Joseph said.

"It makes things a bit strained at the manor." I told him.

"You could always stay here. My parents have plenty of empty bedrooms." He offered.

"I think not." I smiled. "Mr. Sheffield has been a grand host to us. I have an affection for him. He is like a father to me. I like talking to him. He is very smart and he loves God. He is a faith filled man."

"I am happy for you." Joseph said.

"Joseph, what is your relationship to the Almighty?" I asked him.

"That is a very odd question. Everyone I know of believes in God, the creator of the universe. I understand that I am only a man." He replied.

"But that does not answer my question." I told him.

"It doesn't?" He seemed bewildered that I wanted something more.

"No Joseph it doesn't. Do you pray and expect God to answer your prayers? Do you talk to Jesus? Do you value God's opinion of you?" I asked him.

"I pray that you will grow to love me. I would hope that God would want that too and give his approval at our wedding. I suppose I believe that priests should do the informal talking with Jesus, it is more their position in life. As far as God's opinion of me, I'm not sure he is that concerned about my life. With everyone else in the world going through major things I think he is too busy to notice Joseph Carlyle too much." He answered.

"Do you read the bible?" I asked him.

"Lacey, why are you so concerned about my Christianity?"

"It is important to me." I answered.

"Why?" He asked.

"If a man views God as a convenience then he is less likely to believe that he answers to God for his actions. If there is no real respect or consideration or fear of the Lord, then there is no real deterrent to do what is right when no one is looking." I told him.

"You are a very deep thinker Lacey. I live in the real world and have to make real world decisions each day. God is very busy. He doesn't want to be involved with my everyday dealings. I'm an adult. I have to make decisions according to what will suit my life best. You are much too beautiful to worry about such things."

"Do you regard me for my beauty more than my beliefs?" I asked him.

"Lacey, if you want God to be an important part of our lives then I will support you. You can pray and read the bible and go to church on Sunday. I will not interrupt your faith. Raise our children to do the same if you wish. I have no objection." He said.

"Your actions would object to it by your own disregard for giving God his proper place in your life." I argued.

"Lacey please don't make this an issue for us. I love you. I will always be for you and our children. This is causing us unnecessary stress. Please let us go on to other things." He pleaded.

"I think you should kiss me now Joseph." I told him.

He was surprised. "Really? Why in the middle of this discussion do you want me to kiss you?"

"If you don't want to you can dismiss my request." I told him.

"No, I don't want to dismiss your request. I have longed for the chance to kiss you and make up for my past mistakes." He said.

"Well?" I waited.

He leaned toward me and kissed me gently on the lips. I felt nothing at all. There was no connection between us. He took my hand. "Shall we walk?"

"I would like that." I told him.

We spent more time together and it was pleasant enough but there was no more than friendship for me. He dropped me off at home and walked me to the door.

"When can I see you again Lacey?" He asked.

"Joseph, I have tried to open my heart to the possibility of loving you. You have surprised me with your kindness and I have truly forgiven you for what happened. I never wanted you to suffer because of me. I can't love you Joseph. It isn't in my heart and I am sure of it. I believe this situation will never change for me. There is someone out there who will love you like you deserve to be loved, but that person is not me. I don't think we should see each other again hoping that this will change. It will only end up hurting you more and I can't be a part of that." I told him as gently as I could.

"I am very disappointed Lacey. My heart is not ready to let you go, but I will not pressure you at this time. I will walk away like you want me to do. If the opportunity is afforded me to persuade you to marry me, I promise you I will not let it pass. I am grateful that you have made this effort. Goodbye Lacey." He left me at the door.

I walked in relieved that I had survived my promise.

Kurt met me as I was about to walk up the stairs to my room. "Lacey, I'm sorry for the way I've treated you. You didn't deserve to be ignored."

"Excuse me please." I continued up the stairs and ignored his apology.

He watched me walk away and then he went outside to join Ethan and Mr. Sheffield who were talking.

"Lacey is back." Kurt announced as he sat down to join them.

"Did you get a chance to apologize?" Ethan asked him.

"I tried, but she ignored me." Kurt replied.

Mr. Sheffield was amused. "It may take a little extra effort on your part."

"I think he is right. I got off easy because I am her brother and because I didn't waste as much time as you licking my wounds." Ethan said.

Kurt took a deep breath. "Why isn't anything easy?"

Ethan and Mr. Sheffield laughed.

Kurt tried to converse with me at supper. I was polite but I kept my replies short and never looked up at him when I responded.

He walked out on the balcony later when I was standing alone. "Lacey, can we talk?"

"Maybe another time. I'm very tired." I left immediately and went to my room.

He was frustrated with my behavior and his sister knew it. Tricia tried to smooth the way for Kurt while he was working.

"Tricia, please don't get in the middle of this." I said as I walked away from her explanation. I went to the stables and asked Jamison to saddle a horse for me. I rode into town alone and tied my horse to the post just outside the market place. Then I went about looking through the items the vendors had placed on their display carts.

"Lacey, you shouldn't be out here alone." Joseph smiled when he approached me.

I smiled back at him. "I'm fine. It was such a nice day I just didn't want to stay home."

"How did you get here?" He asked.

"I borrowed one of the horses from the stable." I told him as I continued to look over the merchandise for sale.

"May I walk with you?" He asked.

"You really don't have to, but if you want to I have no objection." I told him.

"I would feel better about you having an escort." He said as we walked along.

He was helpful in getting me a better bargain on some items. We talked and laughed together. I didn't feel the pressure of having to have a relationship with him.

"You seem more relaxed around me today." He said.

"You're a nice man Joseph and this is easier for me today. It just feels like you are my friend." I told him.

"Can we be friends?" He asked.

"Why do I feel like if I answer yes then you will view it as an open door to my heart?"

"You know me too well." He admitted as he walked me to my horse.

I got on the horse and he handed me my bags. "It was nice seeing you again Joseph. Thank you for your help and protection."

"Always a pleasure, Lacey." He smiled as I rode away.

When I got home Ethan and Kurt were home from work. Ethan greeted me at the door.

"Lacey, come into the sitting room. We have something to tell you."

I put my bags down near the door and followed him into

the sitting room. Everyone was there including Prentice.

"Kurt and I have found a place for the four of us to share in town. We've explained our plans to Mr. Sheffield and we will be moving out of the manor this Saturday morning." Ethan explained.

I hugged Prentice. "Thank you so much for being so patient with all of us. We can never repay your kindness."

"You have blessed me in more ways than you can imagine. Come to visit me Lacey. I want all of you to visit me. It will be lonely again here." He said.

Kurt and Ethan shook his hand and thanked him. Tricia gave him a hug. We enjoyed the supper meal together. After supper I went on to the balcony. I was going to miss the moonlight over the water and the sound of crashing waves.

Kurt came to stand beside me and I went to leave. "Lacey, please don't keep doing this to me."

"You mean treating you the way you treated me?" I asked him.

"Yes. I'm very sorry it took so long for me to come to my senses." He apologized.

"What you did was childish and selfish. I was afraid to be with Joseph and you abandoned me to it. You shouted your disapproval of me choosing to keep my word every moment you ignored me by your silence. What was I to do? I gave my word. That means something to me even if I am only a woman. You broke my heart to satisfy your own selfish position." I argued.

"I convinced myself to stay out of it for the sake of giving you and Joseph what you promised him, a second chance. I hated every minute you spent with him. I hated that my hands were tied and there was no way to stop it. If I opened my mouth I would have said things that would have made it worse for you. My silence might have been selfish but it was the only way to force myself to stay out of it." He explained.

"There is nothing between Joseph and me. I've told him that I cannot love him. We are not seeing each other because my heart will not allow me to love him. There is no spark that leads me to him and he knows that." I said as I returned to looking out at the ocean.

"Lacey, I'm sorry I'm not better at this." He apologized again.

"Kurt, is there hope for us?" I asked him.

"You ask questions in a way that makes me unsure of what you are asking." He said.

"Nevermind then." I moved away from the stone railing to leave.

He grabbed my hand and gently pulled me closer. "I love you Lacey. If that was what you were referring to, please don't doubt that."

I put my arms around his waist and looked up at him. "I love you too. Joseph had no chance. Even when I made up my mind to sincerely keep my heart open, my heart refused. There is only a place for you there."

He put his arms around me and leaned down and kissed

me. I felt like we completed each other as our lips touched. I didn't want him to stop and when he offered to for a moment, I let him know I wasn't ready to give him up yet.

"So this is why I had no chance?" We heard Joseph's accusing tone as he interrupted us.

I buried my head in Kurt's chest. I didn't want this argument.

"How do you manage to get to her so quickly?" Kurt asked him.

"I came to give her one of the items she dropped at the marketplace today." Joseph answered. "Milton told me she was out here. I never expected to find her in your arms so quickly after she gave me the boot."

"Leave what you brought and go. If Lacey wanted to talk to you, she wouldn't be avoiding you by holding on to me." Kurt told him.

"Lacey, you gave your word that you would give us a good chance. You lied to me. You were just trying to save your brother by your kindness. It was an act." He accused me.

"I can't do this." I whispered.

Kurt moved me behind him to protect me. "Lacey wanted all of us to stay out of your deal. This was the first night she would even have anything to do with me. We both avoided each other so that she could keep her word to you. Whatever happened between you was genuine on her part. She never included me in any of it, not by word or action or deed. You Sir are a spoiled child who cannot take no for an answer. She doesn't love you and you are wearing her out with your personality."

"You have not heard the last of me." Joseph stormed off and out of the manor.

Kurt put his arms around me again to comfort me. "You have affected that man Lacey. I fear he has no intention of giving you up or making it easy on you."

"I'm glad you and Ethan decided that all of us should live together. I would be worried to be alone while you are working. I won't go anywhere alone from now on." I told him.

"That is a very wise decision. Our goal is to go to America and leave him behind. If we stay here he will just keep coming after you." Kurt said.

On Saturday we moved into our three bedroom home. Kurt shared a bedroom with Ethan and Tricia and I got our own rooms. We didn't invest in extra furniture. Our goal was to save enough money to continue our journey to America. Tricia and I looked for a way to make money. There was a restaurant near the harbor called Donovan's. It was owned by Donovan Cross. Tricia and I got a job working there serving the breakfast and lunch meals. We didn't tell our brothers. We worked for a month and made very good tips. We pooled our money together and kept it in a jar under the counter.

Kurt was working and he overheard some of the men talking about two new girls working tables at Donovan's. He stopped working and inquired.

"You mentioned a girl by the name of Lacey?" He asked

one of them.

"Yes, she's very pretty. Do you know her Kurt?"

"I know a girl named Lacey. I'm not sure it is the same girl you mentioned. What is the name of the other new girl?" He asked.

"Tricia." The other man answered. "She's beautiful."

"Long wavy brown hair and green eyes?" Kurt asked.

"Yes, that's her." He answered.

"Watch yourself boys, Tricia is my sister and I am very protective of her and Lacey." Kurt warned them.

"Hey, we've been absolute gentlemen. Donovan would banish us from the place if we stepped out of line with his waitresses. If Tricia is your sister, that is a safe place for her to work."

"Good to know." Kurt went back to working. Just before noon he mentioned going to lunch at Donovan's to Ethan. "It seems our sisters have a job working there as waitresses. We've been kept in the dark and I think we should surprise them."

"Just remember, whatever happens we mind our manners. I've eaten at Donovan's and he serves really tasty food. I don't want to be restricted from the place." Ethan said.

"What would make you think I would be anything other than a gentleman?" Kurt asked.

"Just saying." Ethan said as they walked to Donovan's.

I looked up as they entered the restaurant. "Tricia." I called to her in a whisper. "Tricia!"

She looked my way and I pointed toward the door. She turned around and then turned back to me. "Oh no." She whispered back to me.

Kurt sat down across from Ethan. Tricia approached cautiously. "Hello Kurt. Hello Ethan. What can I get you?"

"Coffee and an explanation would be nice." Kurt said.

"I'll have the same." Ethan told her.

"Coffee it is. I'll be back in a few minutes to take your order. Look over the menu gentlemen." She smiled nervously.

"Hey Lacey, more coffee." One of the men Kurt worked with yelled to me as he held up his cup.

"Be right there Pete." I smiled at him and picked up the pot of coffee to bring to his table. "And how are all you gentlemen today?" I asked politely.

"Much better since we've visited with you Lacey." Pete told her.

"That's the truth." Mike agreed with his friend as I filled his coffee cup.

"It's nice to find pleasant people sitting at one of my tables. Is there anything else I can get for you gentlemen?" I asked.

"Are you free tonight Lacey?" Pete asked.

I smiled at him. "You can pay at the counter."

"Come on Lacey, give a guy a break." Pete said as I walked away.

"I should have a talk with that guy." Ethan said.

"She is handling it. He can't be the only one who is like that to them in here." Kurt said.

"It doesn't upset you?" Ethan asked.

"I'm not going to fight the world. Donovan protects the girls in here. All they have to do is mention that someone is getting out of line and he will handle it. We'll talk to them tonight." Kurt said.

Tricia came back to the table with the coffee. "Have you decided what you would like for lunch?" She looked down at her pad with pencil in hand.

"Tricia, look at me." Kurt whispered.

She looked up at him. "Yes?"

"Are you and Lacey happy with this job?" He asked.

"Yes." She answered.

Kurt smiled and then he ordered his lunch. Ethan gave her his order. She came back and gave it to the cook.

"What did he say?" I asked her.

"He's going to make a big stink about it tonight, I guarantee it." Tricia said.

"He looks happy." I observed.

"It's an act." Tricia said as she grabbed the plates for her other table.

I grabbed my next order and brought it to the table beside them. "Here you go gentlemen." I put the plates down in front of the customers.

"Lacey, could you give us a kiss to go with that coffee? I bet you are a really good kisser." One of them was being fresh.

Kurt started to move and I touched his shoulder. Then I raised my hand and one of the cooks came out of the kitchen and approached my table.

"Is there a problem here Miss Lacey?" He asked me.

"Yes, this man no longer wants to eat here. He would rather insult and embarrass me." I told him.

"Get out!" The cook told him. "Mr. Donovan does not allow anyone to treat his waitresses with disrespect. You will no longer be served at this establishment."

"You're kidding." He objected.

"No Sir, I am not. Don't come back here again. You leave now or Mr. Donovan has instructed me to have you thrown out." The cook said calmly.

The customer threw his napkin down in anger and left.

"Thank you, Ernest." I said.

"Anytime Miss Lacey. We don't need the likes of him."

The cook went back to work.

"Enjoy your meal gentlemen." I smiled and left that table and went on to the next one.

After lunch Kurt returned to work with Ethan. After Tricia and I finished working we decided to cook a very nice supper meal for our two brothers. We dressed up and waited for them to return home from work. They could smell the aroma of the food as they approached the house.

"I think we are being set up." Ethan sniffed the air.

"Smells that way." Kurt smiled.

They walked into the house as we were setting the table.

"Supper will be ready in five minutes." Tricia told them as they came into the house.

Kurt came right to me as I was standing near the stove. He gently turned me around and surprised me with a very nice kiss. My eyes questioned his motive.

"You and I need to talk after supper, privately." He said and then he went to his room to change his clothes and wash up.

They came to the table and sat with us. Ethan blessed the meal and we started to eat.

"Very interesting day Ethan and I had today." Kurt started. "Imagine our surprise when we walked into Donovan's restaurant and found that the two women who are dearest to our hearts were working there as waitresses."

Tricia and I said nothing.

"I for one was shocked that my own sister had not informed me that she had a job, and the girl I've come to love never informed me either." Ethan said.

"It is truly a sad day when you cannot trust a woman to tell you the truth about her day." Kurt said.

I was going to say something and Tricia shook her head no as a warning sign to me.

There was silence at the table as the men waited for us to respond in some way.

"Tricia?" Kurt asked. "Have you nothing to say?"

Tricia shook her head no and kept her eyes down looking at her plate.

"Lacey? Do you have an explanation?" Ethan asked me.

I followed Tricia's lead and did exactly what she did and then I just couldn't hold it together. I started to giggle.

"Your sister seems to think this is funny." Kurt said to Ethan.

"It certainly does appear that way." Ethan was getting aggravated with me.

Tricia wanted me to stop laughing, but I couldn't. I got up from the table and went to our stash of cash under the counter. I brought the can out and placed it in front of Kurt and dumped it over on to the table.

"We wanted to surprise you. We've been working to help raise money to go to America. We were not trying to deceive you. We wanted to surprise you in a nice way." I told them. "One other thing, we are healthy adult women and we don't have to get your permission to do anything. You are brothers, not husbands. I don't ask Ethan for permission and I wouldn't think to ask you because you aren't my husband. We cooked a very nice meal and we would like to enjoy it without being interrogated and treated as if we broke some law."

"Is that how you feel too, Tricia?" Kurt asked his sister.

"We didn't want to cause a problem. We just wanted to help with the passage. The restaurant is a good place to work. The tips are good and we haven't had too many problems. Even Mr. Sheffield has come in to say hello to us. Please don't be upset." Tricia touched Kurt's hand and he pulled it back.

"What goes on between Ethan and Lacey is their business, but you and I have never kept anything from each other. We always discussed things before decisions were made. I don't believe for one minute that your motivation was just to surprise us. You knew that Ethan and I would not want you working in a place that involved flirting with men to obtain money."

"It's not like that." Tricia objected.

"It is exactly like that. I watched both of you. I listened to both of you." Kurt insisted.

"We work hard for that money." I interrupted him. "I don't sell myself and neither does Tricia. How dare you!"

"This is a conversation with my sister." He didn't want to be interrupted.

"It certainly was until you made reference to me. You included me in your lopsided observation. Tricia and I get there early and scrub dishes. We wash tables and chairs. We wash the floors. We run back and forth to tables getting every customer whatever they order and we have to be pleasant during all the complaints and the invitations to spend time with whomever we happen to be serving. It is hard work and we are good at it. Don't you dare narrow it down to selling ourselves for tips. I've been insulted by a lot of people in my life time, but never before have I ever been referred to as a whore by someone I thought I loved." I got up and left the house to go for a walk.

"Lacey wait for me." Tricia threw her napkin down on the table and left with me.

Ethan sat back in his chair. "I've never seen her so angry."

"I didn't call her a whore. Where did she get that from?" Kurt said.

"You said that they flirted with men to obtain money. You said you witnessed it. Kurt, when did that happen? I was there. They were both pleasant and friendly and when they were asked out, they walked away." Ethan said. "What exactly are you angry about? Is it the vast supply of money on the table from their tips? To be honest, Lacey is right. You stepped over the line accusing them of something that just wasn't happening. Tricia didn't deserve it either."

"How long do you think they will be gone?" Kurt asked.

"I think we need to go after them. Lacey won't be watching where she is walking, she's too upset. Tricia won't care where they are going, she will be too involved with the conversation." Ethan said.

"Let's go." Kurt said.

They went outside and looked down the road. "Which direction do you think they went?"

"My guess is that way." Ethan said. "Lacey tends to kick things when she is that angry. Follow the trail of assaulted objects."

They rushed after us.

"There they are. You pull Tricia away so I can talk to Lacey."

Ethan ran up to Tricia. "Sweetheart, can I talk to you alone?"

Tricia stopped and then left with Ethan to walk back home.

"Lacey, I'm very sorry." Kurt apologized.

"Save your apology. It doesn't mean anything to me. What you said was ignorant and mean spirited. We have nothing to talk about." I told him.

"I didn't mean it the way it came out. I don't believe either of you is like a prostitute. The conversation just got out of control. Please Lacey, I'm very sorry that it sounded like that to you. That wasn't what I meant at all." He apologized.

"I don't want to hear your voice. Stop talking to me!" I

yelled at him.

"Please let me walk you home. It is getting dark and it's not safe for you out here alone." He said.

I turned around and headed for home. He walked beside me and didn't say another word. When we got home I went right to my room and he helped Ethan clean up the kitchen and the table with Tricia.

"Tricia, I'm sorry about what I said. I didn't mean it the way it came out. I was upset with all the attention you two girls were getting from the men I work with. I didn't want that for you and Lacey. I overreacted and said it all wrong. I blamed you girls for the way the men were acting toward you. I was upset that we had no idea you were working until today. I tried to figure out why you would keep it from us. Surprising us doesn't explain it all. I still feel that way. There was no reason good enough to keep this from me. I know there is a missing piece, but I had no right to say those things about you and Lacey. I apologize." He said sincerely.

Tricia kissed him on the cheek. "I forgive you, but Lacey won't be so easy to convince. She is insulted and hurt by what you said."

"I know. Tricia, why didn't you tell me? Why didn't you discuss it with me before you went out on your own to find a job? Why didn't you tell me that you worked at Donovan's?" He asked.

"Kurt, please let this go for now. The feathers have been flying around here tonight. Give it a few days to calm down before we talk about it again." Tricia suggested.

"Alright. I'll take your advice." He agreed.

Thursday and Friday I avoided Kurt. I wouldn't talk to him and during our supper meal I ate outside on the stairs. I spent more time alone in my room. Friday night Ethan took Tricia out to a local church social and left Kurt alone in the house with me. I stayed in my room.

"Lacey, please talk to me." He said from outside my bedroom door. "I know I hurt your feelings. I never meant to imply that you sold yourself for money. I used the wrong words. I'm sorry Lacey. Please forgive me. I was just jealous of all the attention you were getting at the restaurant. I didn't want you to be nice to any of them. I know that is no excuse for what I said. I shouldn't have said those things about you or Tricia. It was mean and hurtful. You have a right to be angry with me, but I love you. I was hurt that you kept it from me. I couldn't understand why you wouldn't tell me that you were looking for a job or that you found one. I still don't understand it. I said things that were not true. I was upset and I overreacted. Please Lacey, open the door. I want to fix this between us. Please talk to me."

"Go away." I told him.

"No, I'm not leaving this door until you talk to me. We can't leave it like this. Come out and argue with me if it will help. Just please come out." He pleaded.

I opened the door. "I'm still angry with you."

"I know and I deserve it. Tell me what I can do to make things better and I'll do it." He said.

"I don't know. I never expected you to accuse me of flirting to get money. Really Kurt, think about what you said to me. Out of the abundance of the heart the mouth speaks. You had to have believed it to speak it. You devalued me and your sister with that comment and I believe you meant to say it. I believe you were thinking that very thing well before it came out of your mouth. That's why it hurts so much. You thought about it. You meditated on it and it bothered you to the point of believing it. Then you spoke it to hurt us. At the moment those words left your mouth you showed me that you had no respect for me. You looked at the money I put on the table and it offended your pride somehow. How could two honest, hard working girls make that kind of money without using their beauty or bodies to obtain it? That is what the big question was and you answered it for yourself. You don't love me. You don't even respect me. Please leave my door. I've got nothing more to say to you." I turned to go back into my room.

He grabbed my arm gently. "Lacey, you're wrong. I do love you. I do respect you. How many other men would spend days and weeks living in the same house as the woman they love and never try to take advantage of her? I watch you every day and not once have I ever crossed the line and disrespected you. I've always tried to protect you. I've seen you at your best and at your worst and it doesn't matter, because I love you. You are right. I was angry at the restaurant. I heard Pete ask you out. I heard that man insult you and I wanted to kill him. I watched the other men watching you and I could tell what they were thinking and I hated it. I didn't want you to be friendly to any of them. I was jealous. I wanted to snatch you away from there and forbid you to go back. I heard someone make a comment at the restaurant. That's what started this whole thing. He said if you flirted more you would have gotten a better tip. Then when you spilled all that money on the table, I wasn't happy. I was angry and the two things ran together in my brain. I'm sorry I'm not perfect. I've tried to be a rational, peaceful man around you. Up until now we've never had a real problem. You know we love each other. I know I love you Lacey. I can't promise that I will never hurt you with my words, but I can promise that I will try not to. I certainly will be more careful about your feelings. I don't want to hurt you. I shouldn't have let everything roll together like that. I was wrong. I'm very sorry. Please give me a chance to prove to you that I love you and I respect you."

"Am I going to hear any more objections about Tricia and me working at Donovan's?" I stepped into the hall to ask him.

"As long as no one crosses the line with either of you, I will keep my mouth shut on the subject." He promised.

"I forgive you." I told him.

He hugged me. "Thank you Lacey."

The rest of the evening went well. Saturday morning Tricia and I woke up to the men cooking in the kitchen. They wanted to spoil us with breakfast, right down to the flowers on the table.

"What is the occasion?" I asked Kurt as he pulled out the chair for me to sit on.

Ethan offered a chair to Tricia.

"Are you two up to something?" Tricia asked.

"We just wanted to start this day off right. This is a very important day for all of us." Ethan said.

"Really, why?" I asked.

"Just give us a minute." Kurt put the biscuits on the table.

Ethan put the eggs on the table with the bacon. Then he sat down next to Tricia as Kurt sat down next to me.

We held hands and said grace. Tricia and I started to fill our plates.

"What would you say if I told you that I found a way for us to travel to America for a lot less than we thought it would cost?" Kurt asked as he filled his plate.

"I would say, tell me." I replied.

"I have an opportunity to be a Captain's assistant on the next ship leaving for America." Kurt said.

"And I have an opportunity to work as part of the crew on that same ship." Ethan said.

"That's wonderful. So we won't have to worry about paying for your tickets to America?" Tricia asked.

"Yes and the good news is that once we get to Boston, the ship stays. It was built here, but sold to a company in Boston, Massachusetts. Everyone on the crew is working in order to get to America for free. That way the owners of the ship don't have to pay the standard wage for workers." Kurt said.

"What about Lacey and me? Do you have to pay for a ticket for us?" Tricia asked.

"Lacey you know I love you and Ethan has been in love with Tricia for months." Kurt said.

"That's right Tricia. We talked about getting married. I think we should do that before we leave for America. Will you marry me?" Ethan asked her.

"Yes, of course. I've just be waiting for you to ask me." Tricia hugged him around the neck.

"Lacey." Kurt began.

I knew he was going to ask me at the breakfast table and I didn't want to get a proposal over eggs and biscuits. So I got up and went outside immediately.

Kurt followed me outside. "Lacey is something wrong?"

"Did you give me that whole speech last night just so you wouldn't miss the timing of proposing at breakfast with Ethan?" I asked him.

"No. Last night I was thinking about us and I was sincerely sorry. I didn't want to pressure you into answering a marriage question right after we ended an argument. I was just going to tell you that Ethan wants us to stand up as witnesses for him and Tricia today. He made arrangements with the church to marry Tricia today at two o'clock. He is explaining that to her now." Kurt explained.

"Really?" I was surprised.

"Yes." He answered. "Lacey, when I propose to you, it won't be at a breakfast meal. Come inside and finish your breakfast. I slaved over those eggs."

I took his hand and went back inside.

"Ethan said he arranged for us to get married this afternoon at the church. Isn't that wonderful?" Tricia told me as soon as I sat down.

"Yes it is. Congratulations." I hugged her.

We finished breakfast and then I went into Tricia's bedroom to help her pick out a nice dress to wear. After we had picked out our dresses I excused myself and went downstairs.

I grabbed Kurt by the arm and brought him outside.

"Is something wrong?" He asked me.

"What happens after the wedding?" I asked him.

"I don't know what you mean." He said.

"They will be married Kurt. Your sister and my brother will be married and living in this house with us. They are going to need more privacy than this house can afford them with us living here. What do we do about that?" I asked him.

"Lacey your bedroom is the one furthest away from everything. Just give them your bedroom and you can have Tricia's." He said.

I was frustrated with his answer.

"What?" He asked.

"She is your sister." I said it again.

"And what?" He asked again.

"Don't make me say this." I begged him.

"Lacey, just say it." He waited.

"Tricia is aggressive toward Ethan. She's impatient and loud. She likes the attention. It's not a good idea for either of us to live here after they get married." I told him.

"What are you talking about? She's never been like that." Kurt said.

"Yes she has. She has just been hiding it from you. She won't have any reason to after they are married." I told him.

He wasn't happy. "How long have you been hiding this from me?"

"Tricia and Ethan are just very affectionate. Tricia is my best friend. She loves my brother and they are getting married today. Today Kurt, this afternoon, so don't be upset. Please don't ruin their wedding day. We need to be more concerned with giving them the privacy they need. I suggest we talk to Prentice Sheffield about letting us stay at the manor until we leave for America. When will that be?"

"Don't ask me that now." Kurt didn't want to answer.

"Why not?" I asked him.

"Lacey, give me two days to answer you. Just two days and I promise you will know every detail." Kurt said.

"Alright, but what about Ethan and Tricia? Do you want me to ask Prentice if we can stay at the manor? I'm sure he would love to see us again."

"We'll ask him. We have an hour before we are needed here. Let's take a walk to the manor and invite Mr. Sheffield to the wedding." He took my hand and we walked together talking along the way.

Milton answered the door when we knocked. "Miss Lacey and Mr. Stamos, come in. I will let Mr. Sheffield know you are here."

Mr. Sheffield came to the door to greet us. "Welcome. Come in."

Kurt shook his hand. "It's nice to see you again, Mr. Sheffield."

"We know each other well enough now Kurt for you to call me Prentice. Come into the sitting room and tell me what brings you here." He led the way.

We sat down and I began to explain. "Ethan and Tricia will be getting married at the church today in a little over an hour. He asked her this morning and she said yes. We came to invite you to come and be a guest at the wedding. It will only be the four of us and you. You've been so much a part of our lives here we wanted to invite you."

"I would love to come to their wedding. I understand you are all sharing a house together. It may be difficult for you to do that after the wedding." Prentice remarked.

"We realized that this morning. Prentice would you mind if we gave Tricia and Ethan a few days of privacy and stayed with you at the manor?" I asked him.

"Play the piano for me when you come and you have a

deal Lacey." Prentice smiled.

"I would be happy to." I told him.

"Then it is a deal. Stay as long as you like." He said.

"Thank you so much Prentice." I said.

"Nonsense. You don't need to thank me. It is completely selfish on my part to want you both here. This place is lonely without you." He told us.

"Well, we do appreciate your hospitality." Kurt told him.

"Mr. Sheffield, Mr. Joseph Carlyle is here to see you." Milton announced just before Joseph barged into the sitting room.

Kurt and Prentice stood up at his entrance into the room.

"To what do I owe the honor?" Prentice said.

"I'm sorry for the intrusion Mr. Sheffield, but I found out that Lacey was here and it is urgent that I speak with her alone." He said.

"Lacey, would you like to speak with Mr. Carlyle?" Prentice asked me.

"What is this regarding Joseph?" I asked him.

"Truly Lacey, I believe you would want me to keep this matter private." He said.

"I don't know anyone who has done anything wrong and I haven't done anything wrong, so there is no reason to keep the matter private. Whatever you have to say you can say in front of these two gentlemen." I told him.

"It has come to my attention that your brother Ethan is wanted in England on charges of thievery. My father has a contract with the King's administrator to bring any captured criminals back to England for trial. I came to warn you." Joseph said.

"That is a fabrication. Ethan is an honorable man and has never stolen anything in his life." I insisted.

"He can defend himself when he is returned to England." Joseph said.

"What are you after Joseph? What will it take for you and your father to leave my brother alone?" I asked him.

"Let me speak with you privately on the matter." He suggested.

"Don't do it Lacey." Kurt held my hand. "You can't trust him."

"Lacey, this is your one chance to stop my father from picking your brother up today and hauling him off in chains. Do we talk or not?" Joseph asked.

"Let's go out to the patio." I said to him. Then I turned to Kurt. "I will be fine. I'll return in a few minutes."

Joseph and I walked out to the patio together.

"You know this is a trumped up charge." I accused Joseph.

"Lacey, I've been watching you since you got here. I know all about your job and who you live with. I know about the wedding. The charges are registered and real. There are witnesses. He stole from nobility for your passage to America. I have the power to stop this as long as I get something I've wanted for a very long time, in return." He said.

"What?" I asked.

"You. The ship on which your brother and his wife plan to leave for America is departing in one week. Kurt is leaving with them. All I want is for you to stay behind married to me. I love you Lacey and I've been very patient with you, but my patience is at its end. You stay on the dock and wave goodbye to all of them and Ethan will be left alone. If you deny me, I will put him in chains myself today and he will be gone by the end of the week." Joseph insisted.

"You must give me time to discuss this with Ethan and Kurt." I insisted.

"No Lacey. Make up your mind now or say goodbye to your brother at the jail." Joseph said sternly.

"And if I say yes? What then?" I asked him.

"You attend Ethan's wedding and then you leave with me for my parents' home. I will arrange for the minister to marry us there and by the end of this day you will be my wife. If you are thinking that Prentice can save you from this, you are mistaken. There are things about him that you are not aware of and he will not cross me or my parents. That is why he said nothing when I insisted we speak alone." Joseph informed me.

"Alright, you will have me for your wife." I agreed.

"Say nothing to Kurt or Prentice about this. They will be

informed when you leave with me after the wedding." Joseph insisted. "Lacey, you will kiss me in front of them before we leave that church."

"Is that part of the deal?" I was upset by his command.

"Yes it is. I give you my word that a kiss is all I require until we are married, but do not make the mistake of refusing my affection. I've put up with a lot from you. I am at my limit." He declared.

"Joseph, you are a beast." I said to him.

"I am your beast." He smiled. "Shall we return to the sitting room? Remember, not a word or the deal is off."

We walked back into the sitting room.

"Lacey has invited me to the wedding and I have accepted. We have worked out this day for Ethan. I will be at the church to make sure that he is not arrested. I think it is best that I guarantee his safety." Joseph said.

"What deal did you discuss with Lacey?" Kurt asked.

"It is a private matter between us and shall remain so. Her brother's freedom has been guaranteed by her silence." Joseph said.

"Please excuse us Prentice. We will see you at the church. We have to get back and help Tricia and Ethan get ready for their wedding." Kurt told him.

"I'll be there." Prentice assured us.

"I must leave now and try to stop Ethan's arrest, but I will be at the church to guarantee his safety." Joseph said. "Let me give you a ride back to your house in my carriage. It will save you time."

"No thank you. We will walk." Kurt insisted.

"I'll be right back. I need to use the facilities first." I told them.

"I'll wait for you here." Kurt said.

"I'll meet you at the church." Joseph left.

As soon as I was sure he had left I ran back to Kurt and Prentice.

"Lacey, what's wrong?" Kurt asked.

"Prentice, please help me. Joseph will surely arrest Ethan today if I do not consent to marry him. He plans on taking me from the church today and forcing me to marry him immediately. Then I will be his forever. I wasn't supposed to tell anyone and if he finds out I told you he will take Ethan away. Please tell me you can help us." I begged him.

"I'm not supposed to know any of this, right?" Prentice asked.

"Not a word." I said.

"We have to do this now or you'll have no chance. Go into your home and come out the back door. Make your way to my ship, *The Glory May*. Give these two gold pieces to the Captain. The ship leaves in an hour. I will go to meet you at the church and make excuses about why you are late. Here is a note for the Captain." He scribbled something on a piece of paper. "He will take you to the next port. Get married there. Ethan marries Tricia and I know you love each other. Kurt you marry Lacey. Change your last names for the voyage and take this gold for your passage to America and a new beginning for all of you. Consider it a wedding gift. I expect letters from you once you are settled and safe. Now go before it is too late. Don't pack a bag. Just put layers of clothing on for the voyage." He handed us the bag of gold coins which Kurt tucked away in his vest.

"Thank you Prentice." I kissed him on the lips quickly.

Kurt shook his hand. "Thank you so much."

"Hurry. Look behind you and make sure you are not followed and don't rush back to town. It might raise suspicion." He cautioned us.

Kurt and I walked leisurely back to our home just in case someone was watching. As soon as we got inside the house we informed Ethan and Tricia. Ethan had an idea. He went next door and invited two of our good friends to sneak into our house. He told them what we needed to do and asked for their help. They willingly pretended to be us. I took off my dress and gave it to my neighbor to wear. She changed quickly. Kurt did the same thing with her husband. They walked back and forth in front of the windows quickly to give the impression that we were still home, always keeping their faces out of view.

We left out the back door and kept away from the main road. We made our way to the ship and asked for the Captain. He came to see us and we handed him the note from Prentice.

"Step aboard and let's get to hiding you. We leave port in

twenty minutes." He said.

Kurt handed him the gold pieces that Prentice had specified he was to get.

"I love my job and Mr. Sheffield is a very generous boss. We will take good care of all of you." He promised.

Joseph rode by our home and saw two people moving in the house. He didn't suspect that we were not there. He made his way to the church to wait. Prentice arrived a few minutes later.

"It was very considerate of you to be here to protect Ethan. Lacey told me that your deal with her was fair. She would not tell either of us what it was." Prentice told him. "Why was it so important to keep secret?"

"Lacey is a sweet woman. I have the deepest respect and admiration for her. It was her choice that we keep it secret. I wanted to tell you and Kurt, but she insisted. I was going to offer her another deal, but the one she came up with will make us both happy people. I went with her idea." Joseph told him.

"Very well done." Prentice smiled.

The minister came into the church. "The happy couple should be arriving soon. I had expected to marry two couples, but Mr. Dopolis came by earlier to confirm the ceremony and told me that the other potential groom had lost his nerve and not proposed. So this evening it will only be him and Miss Stamos that wed. Are you friends of the bride or the groom?"

"Both." Prentice replied.

"They seem to be running a little late." The minister said.

"That has to be Tricia. She has a habit of changing her mind at the last minute. Please wait. I'm sure they will be here very soon." Prentice told them as he checked his watch. He realized his ship had just left with all of us hidden away.

Our neighbors grabbed whatever was of value in our home and moved it to their own quickly. It was a gift from us to them for their help. We warned them to hide the items for at least a week.

After ten minutes Prentice acted concerned. "A little late is one thing. Something must have happened to them. I should go and check at their house. Please Reverend, wait until I get back. I'll bring them with me. Just give me another ten minutes. I hope Ethan and Tricia have not changed their minds about getting married."

"I'll wait ten more minutes." The minister agreed.

"I'll go with you Mr. Sheffield. Maybe I can help with something." Joseph offered.

Each of them raced to our home. Prentice knocked on our door and no one answered. "Well, we didn't pass them along the way. Where could they be?"

Joseph was visibly angry. He pounded on the door. "Open up!" He yelled.

Our neighbor was careful to change out of Kurt's clothes before he came out of his house. "Are you looking for the people who lived there?"

"What do you mean, lived there?" Prentice asked.

"Well, they packed up about twenty minutes ago and left." He said.

"How did they leave?" Joseph asked.

"Looked like a wagon to me. The big guy, Kurt, seemed to know the owner of the wagon. They stuffed their things on it and the owner drove them away." He explained.

"Which way did they go?" Joseph asked.

"That way." He pointed.

"I don't understand. Why would they leave? Sir, did they mention anything to you before they left?" Prentice asked.

"No, nothing at all." He said.

"Well, I guess I'll go home and wait for them to contact me." Prentice said. "This is so odd."

"I want to know if they contact you. I can't protect Ethan if I don't know where he went." Joseph said.

"Absolutely right. As soon as I know anything I will let you know. I'm going back to the church to tell the minister what we found out. Goodnight Joseph. Give my regards to your parents." Prentice left.

"Ladies and Gentlemen, please join me in my quarters for supper. We will be pulling into the next port in three days. It is a little bit of a detour off our normal route, but you can catch a boat to America there. That is what Mr. Sheffield wanted and he gets what he wants." The Captain told us.

We came out of hiding and followed the Captain. We walked along the deck and all we could see was ocean.

"We are safe Lacey." Kurt said as he walked with me.

"It feels wonderful to be safe." I replied.

"Lacey, before we join the Captain can I talk to you for a minute?" Kurt asked.

"Sure." I stepped to the side of the ship as Kurt told the Captain we would be joining him in a few minutes.

Kurt joined me. "Lacey, you know I love you. Prentice was right. We have to change our last names, but we have an opportunity now to be completely free from the past. First, I want to ask you to marry me. Will you marry me Lacey?"

"I love you. Yes, I would love to marry you." I told him.

"Lacey, I think we should have the Captain marry us at sea, all of us. That way we can use our correct names and do it right. Then I think we should all get married as soon as we land with our new names. I think we should change both our first and last names and start completely new. In America a name means something. The last name I mean. Let's really think about this before we change our names. We change our names and where we came from. Every part of our lives can be different and that will guarantee that Joseph can never track down Ethan or make trouble for you again. If there are charges against Ethan they will never find him. The Captain can give us documents with our names on it. Work papers for all of us. Then we get married and we have it recorded. We can be completely free. What do you think about that?" He asked.

"I think it is a wonderful idea." I agreed.

"Let's go talk it over with the Captain." Kurt suggested.

I took his hand. "Let's."

We sat down to supper with the Captain. He blessed the meal and we began eating.

"You four are very special to Mr. Sheffield. Is there anything I can do for you while you are in my care?" The Captain asked.

"We would like you to marry us at sea." Kurt said.

"That would be wonderful." Ethan agreed.

"Very well. We will marry you tomorrow morning. Would you like the crew to witness it or keep it private among yourselves?" He asked.

"Private." Kurt said.

"I will perform the marriage ceremony in my quarters after sunrise." He offered.

"There is one other matter Captain." Kurt said.

"Yes, what is it?" He asked.

"Mr. Sheffield suggested that each of us change our names. We will need work documents listing those new names. Can you supply those for us?" He asked.

"That shouldn't be a problem for you two men; however I will have to write up passage documents for the ladies." He said.

"Thank you so much. We will discuss our new names this evening and let you know what we have chosen after you marry us. Our intention is to get married on land before we leave for America, using our new names." Kurt explained.

"And have the marriage recorded?" The Captain smiled.

"Yes Captain." Kurt replied.

"That is a very good plan." The Captain agreed.

"Yes that is a very good plan." Ethan said as he looked at Tricia.

After supper we discussed the culture in America and what names might work best for us. Kurt chose the last name of Albert for himself. Ethan chose the last name of Bernard for himself. They reasoned that those last names came from more than one nationality and they could use the diversity to blend into whatever community they needed to. Tricia and I decided that our maiden names would be descriptive. I chose Stands and she chose Grace. Then we decided to pick names that were closest to the ones we already had so that if we slipped up talking to each other we would be able to explain it easily. Tricia became Patricia Grace, Ethan became Athan Bernard, Kurt became Curtis Albert and I changed my name to Lais Stands. We thought they were perfect.

The next morning we met the Captain for breakfast and told him our new names. He was amused by the situation. "I would suggest that after I marry you, you start calling each other by your new names. That will give you two days to get used to them before we drop you off. We won't be exchanging rings here, so in lieu of that you will kiss your brides after I pronounce you man and wife. The crew already believes you are married. I informed them after we were at sea. It is better that way. It keeps the men away from the ladies."

"Thank you Captain." I said.

"Breakfast is finished. Let's go to my quarters so that we can make this legal." The Captain stood up.

We followed him into his quarters and he performed our wedding ceremonies. We enjoyed the kiss that sealed the deal. Then he wrote out our identification papers with our new names on them. "Keep these in a safe place. Congratulations to you all. I'm sorry that your wedding night accommodations are not more private. I do have some cash on board. I can exchange a few of your gold coins for currency. It may be easier for you and not expose you as wealthy people just yet."

"We appreciate all that you have done for us Captain." Kurt said. He handed over a gold coin which the Captain exchanged for currency.

Ethan did the same.

"Feel free to roam the deck. Mr. Albert, make sure you point out the dangers to your wife. Mr. Bernard, you do likewise." The Captain instructed.

Two days later we arrived at our first destination. The Captain had provided us with bags to carry our clothes. Our first stop was at a merchant shop to purchase luggage to carry our personal items. Our next stop was to purchase wedding bands. Ethan bought one for Tricia and Kurt bought one for me. We didn't want to bring attention to ourselves and simple was better. Then we sought out a Judge to marry us. The ceremony had a lot less substance than our first one with the Captain, but it was legal and recorded. The Judge wrote out a certificate of marriage for both couples and we all left together. I was now Mrs. Lais Albert and Tricia was now Mrs. Patricia Bernard.

Kurt and Ethan got us rooms at the local Inn. Tricia and I decided to rest while Kurt and Ethan went to the Port Master and booked us the best tickets on the *Grand Bateau* which was leaving for America in two days. This time we would not have to share our space with a large group of people. We were able to reserve a room on the ship that we only had to share with Ethan and Tricia. We were very grateful for the luxury the gold coins from Prentice had afforded us.

When Kurt got back to our room at the Inn, I was sleeping. He climbed into bed next to me and fell asleep. He needed the rest too. When I woke up he was still asleep. I left the room quietly and went to Ethan's door and knocked on it.

He cracked the door so I could see his face. "Lacey? What is it?"

"Can I talk to you for a minute?" I whispered.

"Where is Kurt?" He asked.

"Sleeping. Ethan it's important." I whispered.

He rolled his eyes. "Alright. Give me a minute." He shut the door.

I could hear Tricia ask him who it was at the door and I

heard him reply to her that it was me.

"What does she want?" Tricia asked.

"I have no idea. I'll just be a minute." He said. He met me in the hall two minutes later. "Lacey, what is so important?"

"Ethan, Kurt will be awake soon. What happens now?" I asked him.

He was shocked by my question. "Lacey, you need to ask your husband that question." He whispered as he turned me around by my shoulders. "Every man has a plan for his marriage. I explained those things to my wife and Kurt will explain those things to you. Go ask him. It is not my place to answer questions about your marriage." Then he gave me a little push. "Go ask him."

I went back to my room and sat in the chair near the bed until Kurt woke up.

He sat up in the bed. "Mrs. Albert what are you doing sitting in that chair?"

"I have a dilemma." I answered.

"And what would that be?" He asked.

"I went to Ethan's room and asked him a question and he said I should ask you. He insisted on it." I explained.

"What question?"

"What happens now?"

He smiled at me. "Lacey come here and sit with me on the

bed."

I got up and went to the bed to sit next to him.

"This is the first chance we've had to be alone and relaxed. I've missed out on being with my wife." He brushed my hair gently off my shoulder and then he kissed me. "We are about to discover together what happens next."

Chapter Seven

Two days later we were boarding the *Grand Bateau* for our trip to America. I was a little nervous as we found our room.

"Do you think we will survive this?" I asked Kurt.

"I looked over the ship. They have everything they need to make the voyage a safe one. I promise to protect you Lacey. Please relax. I'm sure we will make it this time." He said.

We stayed in our room as the ship pulled out into open water. Kurt hugged me for ten minutes just so I would feel safe.

"We should go and walk the deck. We have quite a few days on this ship. Fresh air will make you feel better about the travel." He said.

I agreed and went upstairs with him. We met Ethan and Tricia near the back of the ship and told them that we had already put our things in the room. We gave them directions to it.

"I think we are all a little nervous about this voyage." Ethan said. "I've got my knife attached to my belt and I brought a rope."

"You're going to make Lacey more nervous than she is already. Just stop talking about it. Let's take this time to make connections. It is a wise thing to meet the people on board. Our room is in a good place." Kurt said.

"Most of them speak French." Tricia remarked.

"Well I will be lost in that conversation." I told them.

"I'll translate for you." Kurt offered.

"You speak French?" I was surprised.

"I told you, I worked on ships. I've been in and out of harbors and among a variety of crew members. I know some French and some Spanish." He explained.

Tricia laughed. "He is telling stories. We had an uncle who married a French woman. She taught Kurt and me how to speak French when we were growing up because she wanted to be able to talk to us. He just brushed up on it a little more on the ships."

"So you know it too?" I asked her.

"Yes she does." Ethan answered before he kissed her on the cheek.

I got the romantic reference he was making. "Well, let's go mingle."

"We need to go to the room first and put our things away. We will meet you later." Ethan told us.

We went off in different directions. Kurt introduced himself and spoke on subjects concerning the ship and how it handled. That attracted those who wanted to find someone they could trust to keep them informed. When Tricia started to mingle she met people by complimenting mothers on how well behaved or cute their children were. Each of them translated to Ethan and me. Occasionally, we met people who spoke very good English. By the end of the first week there was a large number of people who knew us by name. It made the voyage very enjoyable for all of us.

Finally the day came when the Boston harbor was spotted in the distance.

"There it is Lacey, our new home." Kurt was standing behind me and had his arms wrapped around me as the wind blew across the bow of the ship.

I felt sad about my parents. They missed out on the new life they had planned to have in America. I could feel tears running down my cheeks. I wiped my eyes and Kurt suddenly noticed.

"Are you crying, Lacey?" He asked me.

"I'm just sad that my parents didn't get a chance to see this." I told him.

"Me too. My Dad talked about America for years before he bought the tickets to come here. If we have a few boys we are going to name them after our fathers."

"We'll talk about that later." I said.

"Don't you like your father's name?" He asked me.

"I love my father's name. It's your father's name I don't

care for." I told him.

"You don't like Herman for a name for our son?"

"I'm sorry Kurt, but Herman Albert sounds awful." I answered.

"It sounds fine." He insisted.

"We'll talk about it later. I'm not even pregnant. We have plenty of time to pick names. Let's not fight about it now."

"You're right. This discussion can be postponed." He agreed.

"What is the first thing we do when we get off the ship?" I asked him.

"Our names are changed and only my Dad kept in touch with the relatives. Without his introduction they won't believe I am related to them, so we are pretty much on our own. We need to find a place to live and I need to find a job." He said.

One of the passengers approached us as we were standing there. "I'm sorry, but I overheard your conversation and I may be able to help."

Kurt knew who he was. "We would appreciate your advice, Mr. Beckman."

"I hate these voyages. I have to make them once a year for business reasons. I live in Boston with my wife and three children. I own a manufacturing business and I need a man who can speak French as well as English. We have an import/export situation on the docks. I need a man to oversee that part of the business as a foreman. You're certainly strong enough to do the labor and since you speak French, translation with the people I have to deal with will be easy for you. The job pays well and I can help you find a place to live. Are you interested?" He asked Kurt.

"Absolutely!" Kurt shook his hand.

"Then follow me when we get off the ship." Mr. Beckman told him.

"Thank you Sir." Kurt said.

"You're very welcome. Curtis, I haven't been introduced to your wife yet."

"I'm so sorry for my bad manners. Mr. Beckman this is my wife Lais."

"It is very nice to meet you Mrs. Albert." Mr. Beckman said politely.

"It is a pleasure to meet you too, Mr. Beckman." I smiled.

"I noticed you were staying with family during the voyage. You can bring them along too. What skills does your brother have?" He asked.

"Athan is an exceptional carpenter. He can design and build anything you want or need." Kurt told him.

"I'll find a place for him too. Bring them along with you. As soon as the boat docks make sure you are all behind me. The crowd will be thick when we get off the ship. Protect your wives and push through. I'll meet you here in twenty minutes." He said.

"We'll be here." Kurt assured him.

Mr. Beckman left and we rushed to find Ethan and Tricia. We told them about the job offer and all of us rushed back to our room and gathered up our things immediately. We went directly back to the spot Mr. Beckman had told us to meet him.

Twenty minutes later Mr. Beckman was standing next to us with his luggage.

"Mr. Beckman, this is my brother-in-law, Athan Bernard and his wife Patricia." Kurt introduced them.

"Very nice to formally meet you both." He smiled.

"We really appreciate this opportunity Mr. Beckman." Ethan told him.

"Do you speak French too?" He asked Ethan.

"No Sir, only my wife and Curtis have that skill." He replied.

"Mrs. Bernard, can you teach your husband the language?"

"I'm sure over time he can learn it. Will it be necessary for this employment?" She asked.

"In time it may be. You start on it as soon as you can. It will be a value to him in his future." Mr. Bernard replied.

"Yes Sir, we will get started as soon as we are settled." Tricia promised.

"Very well then. Now stay close, push through, and

protect your wives. There will be a carriage for us once we get through the crowd. If we get separated I will stand up in the carriage. Look for me. I'm not a very patient man, so make sure you hurry. I don't like to be kept waiting." He told us. "If you have money don't keep it in your pants pockets. There are thieves who will bump into you and steal it before you know it is gone."

"We've already taken care of that." Kurt told him.

"I knew you were smart." Mr. Beckman smiled.

"Lacey, you hold on to me no matter what. If we lose luggage, don't worry about it. Everything we have can be replaced in time. You and having a job are more important than what is in that bag." Kurt told me.

"Tricia, he is right. Hold on and don't let go of me." Ethan told her.

Once we reached the dock it was insane. People were pushing and thieves were in the crowd to steal from the passengers coming off the boat. It seemed a miracle that we made it through and never lost sight of Mr. Beckman. There was a large carriage waiting for him with a driver. It was big enough to hold our luggage and the five of us with his driver.

Mr. Beckman sat in front with the driver. He turned to us as Ethan and Kurt were helping Tricia and me to climb into the seats. "I find some of the best men to work for me on those voyages. That is why my driver brings the larger carriage along. Let's get you settled first."

We were ready for the trip as the driver pulled away from

the people. It took about five minutes to reach the housing area.

"Kurt, will we be able to afford this?" I whispered to him.

"We've been blessed so far. We have the gold coins Prentice gave us. If it gets too expensive for us we can move." He whispered.

"The apartments are small, but this is a very safe area. You are welcome to look for another place at any time. I just wanted to start you off in a section of town that was close enough to my business and safe enough for your wives." Mr. Beckman told our husbands.

The driver stopped the carriage and we got down. Mr. Beckman was handed the keys to the apartments by his driver. He handed Kurt a key and gave another one to Ethan. "The number of your apartment is on the key. Go check it out and if you like it your wives can stay here while I show you both where you will be working and what will be expected of you."

"Mr. Beckman, how much is the rent on the apartment?" Kurt asked him.

"It will cost you one fifth of your pay as long as you live here. As your pay goes up so does your rent. Some of the men who have lived here with their families find the arrangement unfair after a few months and they find another place. That is your choice. This can be the place you start out in or you are welcome to stay. It is your choice, but it will always cost you one fifth of your pay." He explained.

Kurt and Ethan left us near the carriage and went into the

apartments to check them out. The apartments had a kitchen, a living area and a bedroom. They looked out the back window and could see the area where the outhouses were built. They were a bit of a walk, but they looked to be in good shape.

Kurt came outside to talk to Mr. Beckman. "Where do we get water?"

"That small shed has the water pump inside. Only the tenants have the key to the shed. Once you say yes to the apartment I will give you the key." He said.

"Are there any rules about the outhouses?" He asked.

"Each two units share an outhouse. Your family will share the one built behind your units. There is no lock on the door, but I would suggest that you find a way to lock it so that vagrants won't think this is a section of town to take advantage of. You will find your neighbors have already taken that measure to insure that they will not be surprised when a need arises." He told us.

"Thank you Mr. Beckman. We certainly appreciate your accommodations. We are grateful for the apartments. If we plan to move in the future, what is required?" Kurt asked him.

"One month's notice from the date your payment is due, which will be on the first of the month. I warn you ahead of time that if you do not give notice I will take the next month's payment out of your check or take you to court for it and they always decide in my favor." He explained.

"We understand." Kurt said.

"And if the job doesn't work out?" Kurt asked.

"If you are fired and you have already paid for the month then you will stay to the end of it. If you quit, you have the same option. Only employees of mine can stay at these apartments." He explained.

"Lacey, we have a home." Kurt told me.

"Patricia, we also have a home." Ethan told her.

Mr. Beckman handed our husbands each a key to the water shed. "Bring your things in and leave the ladies. I have to show you where you will be working tomorrow."

They did as he instructed. Kurt kissed me goodbye and told me to lock the door with or without Tricia. He promised to be back as soon as he could. Ethan did the same. We watched them leave with Mr. Beckman.

Tricia and I locked our doors and started to put our things away. We were fine for the first hour and then one hour turned into two hours. Tricia left her apartment and knocked on my door.

"Lacey, I'm worried. They have been gone so long. I can't stay with you because Ethan has the key to lock the door from the outside." She said as she stood in my doorway.

"Let's not panic. Kurt and Ethan are very smart and very strong. They won't let anything keep them from us. Go back into your apartment and believe that. Say a prayer for them. They will be back. You know they will." I was trying to convince myself of it as I said it.

"Alright. I will pray for us." Tricia said as she left my doorway and went back into her apartment and locked the door.

I made sure to lock mine. I sat on the floor and waited.

About an hour later a supply wagon pulled up in front of our apartments. Kurt jumped out of the back of it with Ethan. We saw them at the same time and ran outside to meet them.

"Lacey, Mr. Beckman let us borrow the wagon so that we could buy furniture and other items for our apartments. He let his driver take us around town." He handed me some food. "Ethan and I will unload the wagon while you and Tricia cook us something to eat."

Ethan was explaining the same thing to Tricia. We were both surprised and relieved, but emotionally wrecked. We tried not to show our emotions as we went into my home to prepare a supper meal for our husbands, but as we were going about doing that both of us started to whimper and wipe our tears with relief.

Ethan was carrying in his furniture with Kurt's help. They stopped when they heard us.

"What's going on?" Ethan asked Kurt.

"I have no idea." He answered.

"Do we check? We only have a limited time to use the wagon." Ethan reminded him.

"Let's run in and give them a quick hug and kiss. Then we will talk to them after we are done. Make it quick." Kurt said as they put down what they were carrying.

Ethan came into my home, turned Tricia around and

hugged her quickly and kissed her. "I don't know why you are crying and I'm sorry that you are, but we have a limited time to use the wagon."

She was still crying. "Do what you have to."

Kurt got the same response from me. Then he joined Ethan to unload the rest of the furniture as quickly as possible. When they were finished they thanked the driver and tipped him with some money. They watched him drive away. Then Ethan locked up his apartment and joined us in ours for supper.

Tricia and I were wiping our eyes when we sat down to eat. We were still wavering between worry and relief. Our husbands pulled us into their laps.

"What is going on with you girls?" Ethan asked.

"You were gone so long, we worried that something happened to you." Tricia explained.

"We worried about what we would do if you didn't return to us." I explained.

"Ethan and I would never let anything or anyone stop us from getting back to you." Kurt tried to reassure us.

"We are here now. You have a nice home and food on the table and we have very good jobs. Concentrate on that for now." Ethan said as he held Tricia close to him.

"Please relax, both of you. Ethan is right. We are very well off and safe. Please try not to worry anymore." Kurt kissed me on the cheek. "Lacey, take a deep breath and relax.

I'm never going to leave you."

Tricia and I went back to our chairs and we all held hands while Kurt blessed the meal. Then we ate and it was delicious. Tricia helped me clean the table while Ethan helped Kurt put the bed together.

"Lacey, get ready for bed. It's been a long day. I'm going next door to help Ethan put their bed together, then I will be back." Kurt kissed me and left with them, locking the door as he went.

We had two windows in the front of our little dwelling and another few windows on the side and back. I went through our supplies of blankets and sheets and managed to cut up a sheet and nail panels of it up against the windows so that we could have privacy. I was still banging the hammer when Kurt returned from Ethan's house.

"I expected you to be waiting in bed for me." He said as he approached the chair I was standing on.

I looked down at him. "I needed privacy first. I didn't want our neighbors spying on us."

"Good point, but it is too bad you had to cut up that new sheet." He helped me off the chair after I finished my work.

"Watch me out the back door for a minute. I have a personal trip to make." I told him.

"Ladies first." He reached into his pocket and gave me the key to the lock he had put on the outhouse.

"Thanks." I left through the back door as he stood in the

doorway watching for me. I handed him the key when I returned. "I hope you have two of those."

"We only need one and we will keep it on this nail by the back door. Now get dressed for bed." He said before he went out the back door and shut it behind him.

Chapter Eight

    The next morning we heard a rooster announce the morning. Everyone in Mr. Beckman's little community started to get ready for work. An empty supply wagon was driven into the street outside our home about thirty minutes later. Kurt gave me a kiss goodbye warning me that he wouldn't return for at least ten hours, possibly more. He handed me the house key before he left. I peeked out the window and saw Ethan get into the back of the wagon beside Kurt. Then the driver pulled away to head back to the ships.

    I climbed back in bed knowing that Tricia and I were much better off today than yesterday. We had the keys to our homes and the water shed. After I rested for another hour I got up and started to put away our clothing in the bureau Kurt had bought for us. Around eight o'clock that morning I knocked on Tricia's door.

    "Good morning Lacey." She smiled at me when she opened the door.

    "I was wondering if you were up to doing a little shopping today? I have sheets instead of curtains and Kurt did not think to buy me a sewing machine."

    "I would love to. Come inside and check out our home."

She invited me.

I locked up my little house and took her up on her invitation. Her things were slightly different from mine, but very nice. We left a few minutes later to walk through parts of Boston that we hadn't seen yet.

"Make mental notes of our way back to our homes. I don't want to get lost." I told her.

"I think we should do this gradually. Let's not go too far all at once." Tricia said.

"There is our street sign. We have to remember what street we are on. At least if we get lost someone might be able to point us in the right direction." I told her.

The people seemed polite enough. We walked through a market place and talked with some of the merchants. They were very nice, but did not have a lot of time to spend on one customer. There were a few stores along the way. We held on to our purses tightly and we were very aware to be extra cautious if someone bumped into us. Kurt had warned us about pickpockets. We found the material we liked to make curtains out of. We didn't want to venture far enough to find a sewing machine, so we opted for sewing supplies. Then we bought food items so that we could make supper together again for our husbands. We were happily returning to our homes when two teenage boys offered to carry our items for us.

"No thank you." I replied to their offer.

"It's no trouble Miss. We can see that you have your

hands full." The tallest one got closer.

"We are fine. Just be on your way." Tricia said forcefully.

We thought we were going to have trouble, then we heard the voice of someone behind us. "Leave the ladies alone!"

The two boys scattered. We turned around to see a slightly older boy standing behind us.

"They'll not be troubling you again." He tipped his hat to us.

"Thank you." Lacey said.

"Will you be causing us trouble?" Tricia asked.

"No Mrs. Bernard." He answered.

"How do you know me?" Tricia asked.

"Mr. Albert and Mr. Bernard found me yesterday and offered me a business opportunity." He explained.

"Which is what?" Tricia asked him.

"I make sure no one bothers you when you are about doing your business. Allow me to introduce myself. My name is Sam O'Bean. I've been living on the streets of Boston by my wits for years. I do odd jobs for cash, shelter and meals. Your husbands knew you would be shopping today and they hired me to watch over you. Once I walk you home will you be staying there the rest of the day?" He asked.

"Yes." I answered.

"That's good because I have other jobs I've been hired to

complete. Tell your husbands of my service to you today and I'll be stopping by about supper time to pick up my meal for the day. What time would that be?" He asked.

"We really aren't sure. This is their first day of work." I told him.

"They work for Beckman?" He asked.

"Yes." I answered.

"I would be counting on eating about half past six. I'll be on your doorstep then. You don't have to invite me in. Just give me a plate and a drink and when I am done I will leave it at your back door." He said.

"Of course you are invited to join us." I told him.

"I beg your pardon Mrs. Albert, but I would suggest you clear that with your husband first. He may have his reasons for keeping me out of your home. I will not be offended by it. His duty is to you first. If he says it is alright, I would be happy to come in and join you. If he would rather I take my meal outside that is perfectly fine too. Please let him decide." He said politely. "I would offer to carry some of your things, but you don't know me yet and to say yes to such an offer would be unwise until you do."

We carried our own things the rest of the way. Sam walked us to our doors and said goodbye when we went inside. Tricia and I worked on the curtains until they were done. Then we realized we had no way to hang them up without nailing them. We didn't want to ruin our good work, so we folded them and put them aside for another day.

We started to prepare supper and made sure that we made enough to share with Sam O'Bean.

Ethan and Kurt got home a few minutes before six o'clock. They walked in the house tired and dirty from a day's work. Both of them grabbed the water bucket inside the door and went to the shed to fill it. Then they came back inside and grabbed the soap and a towel.

Kurt went into the bedroom to wash up while Tricia and I finished setting the table. He came out in clean clothes and looking refreshed. Ethan joined us a few minutes later.

"Kurt, a young man by the name of Sam O'Bean came to our rescue today. He will be here soon to collect his supper meal. Can he join us inside?" I asked him.

"Not tonight." Kurt said.

"Why is that?" I asked him.

"I don't trust him." Kurt replied. "When he comes, I'll take his supper meal to him."

Just then there was a knock on the back door.

Kurt grabbed the plate I had ready for Sam with his drink and opened the door. He went outside and handed it to him. "I heard you rescued my wife and sister today."

Sam took the plate and made himself comfortable on the ground next to the house. "It was my pleasure to come to the aid of those fine ladies."

"You set it up, didn't you?" Kurt accused him.

"That would be dishonest." Sam replied indignantly.

Kurt laughed. "I used to be you. You aren't fooling anyone here. I saw you asking around last night about us. I won't be played the fool, but I do appreciate a man with ingenuity. You watch over my wife and my sister from now on for real and I'll make sure you get a supper meal each night for you and your two friends. If you let me down don't come around again."

"I do appreciate that Mr. Albert." Sam smiled.

"Just don't cross me." Kurt warned him.

"It will never happen Mr. Albert. I swear on the life of my beloved mother." He said sincerely.

Kurt laughed. "I did some checking too Sam, and you have no mother. You've been living on these streets for years with your two friends. I check out the people who check me out. The warning stands. If you jeopardize the two people I care about most, I promise you will regret it."

"Well said Mr. Albert. Well said." Sam went back to eating his meal and Kurt started to come back inside.

"Sam, give me a minute and I'll get you a plate for the other boys who are hiding near here." Kurt smiled. He stepped inside. "Lacey, make up another plate with two drinks."

I did what he asked and he took it out to the two boys who had joined Sam. They were grateful.

"Be careful not to bite the hand that feeds you

gentlemen." Sam was heard saying as Kurt came back inside to join us.

Kurt sat down at the table and filled us in on the set up. "We have to be careful around here. There are a lot of people who don't have money or work. I think it's wise that we get to know our neighbors. If they need help, Ethan and I will offer a kind hand. You don't share personal items, food, money, or property unless you speak to Ethan or me first. I don't care what the situation is. If you want to visit with the other women do it outside in the open. I don't want anyone in this house until we are more acquainted with the people we live around." He told us.

Tricia looked at Ethan for his word on it.

"I think Kurt is being wise. We don't want to invite trouble. Boston has a police department. If it is a real issue we can report the matter to them." Ethan told her.

Tricia and I agreed to follow the instructions of our husbands.

"Don't go anywhere alone and don't carry so much that your hands are full. As sneaky as Sam was about the set up, he made a good point. He will be watching out for you and when he steps in I want to know. From now on he eats supper when we do. Buy enough to share with him and his two friends. Any other compensation I will work out with them if I choose to." Kurt said.

The boys finished their meal and stacked the plates and the glasses at the back door. Then they left.

"Do you think they have a place to sleep at night?" I asked Kurt.

"Lacey, you are not their mother. That young man can take care of himself. He has to be at least sixteen. He is smarter than he looks." Kurt said as he stood up to clear off his spot.

A few months later Mr. Beckman surprised Kurt at the dock.

"Mr. Beckman, it's so nice to see you again Sir." Kurt greeted him with a handshake.

"I hear good things about your management skills down here Curtis. Your brother-in-law does good work too." Mr. Beckman remarked as they walked.

"That's nice to hear. Is there another reason you came to the dock today?" Kurt asked him.

"Actually yes. I have a proposition for you." Mr. Beckman stopped walking and looked directly at Kurt.

"Yes Sir?" Kurt waited.

"I'll be exporting items to the south. I can find a good replacement for you here in Boston. There are experienced men coming off the ships daily. My concern is that I can't find anyone as experienced and dependable as you at sea. The pay would be three times what you make now, but you would be at sea for weeks, possibly months." He said.

"I don't understand. Even if you exported items by ship to the south, the journey wouldn't take weeks. It is simply the coastline." Kurt said.

"I'm in a partnership with a man from North Carolina. I supply the ship and the crew and he takes them across the ocean to pick up slaves. We transport those slaves to North Carolina and the profit we make has the potential to make us all very rich." Mr. Beckman said.

"I'm sorry Mr. Beckman, but I am not the man for the job. I don't support slavery in any form. I cannot be a part of it." Kurt told him.

"I'm very disappointed Curtis. I had high hopes for you and your future here. You are leaving me short handed and ill equipped to hold up my end of the deal. It will take me time to find someone I trust to represent me in this venture. You have the skills that I need for this job. You could cost me this business arrangement." Mr. Beckman wasn't happy.

"I understand your situation, but I cannot be your representative on this matter." Kurt held his ground.

"Carry on with what you have been doing. I will look elsewhere for the person I need." Mr. Beckman assured him.

"Thank you Sir." Kurt replied as Mr. Beckman walked away.

A few hours later Sam O'Bean was knocking on my back door.

"Sam, is there something I can help you with?" I asked him.

"Mrs. Albert, your family is in a big bit of trouble." Sam

warned.

"What kind of trouble?" I asked him.

"The, *get out of here*, kind of trouble." He said.

"Why?" I asked him.

"Mr. Albert made Mr. Beckman very angry. Your husband turned down a job offer from Mr. Beckman and Mr. Beckman isn't about to take no for an answer. He has men of unsavory character plotting to force Mr. Albert to take the job. I'm worried about you and Mrs. Bernard. You have to leave here quickly. Your husband told me to protect you both and I'm trying my best to do that. It's not safe for you to be here alone. I can take you and Mrs. Bernard to a safe place and return you when your husbands get home." Sam offered.

"Sam, I can't leave here with you. I have to wait for my husband." I insisted.

"At least stay with Mrs. Bernard in the same house. If there is trouble my boys can cause a distraction and I might be able to get you away from here. We'll be hanging about. If I spot trouble I will come to the back door to get you both." He promised.

"Alright. I'll stay with Tricia." I agreed.

"Use the back door Mrs. Albert." Sam urged me.

I took my key and locked the back door. As soon as it was locked, Sam covered my mouth and his friends helped him to carry me away from my home. Tricia had no idea that I was gone. They took me into the woods and tied me up and gagged my mouth.

"Now Mrs. Albert, I wouldn't do this awful thing to you if I wasn't trying to protect you. Please believe me. You've been so good to me and my boys. We are going to cover you with this blanket. Now you be still while we bring Mrs. Bernard here. Once your husband gets home we will tell him where you are." Sam tried to be reassuring, but I didn't trust him and I was afraid for Tricia.

They covered me with the blanket and left. About fifteen minutes later they were doing the same thing to her. They uncovered me to see her.

"Sam is right, Mrs. Albert." The youngest one, named Gus said. "You are all in danger."

"If we wanted to take something from you we would have taken your keys and went through your house. We are just trying to protect you. We don't want to keep you tied up and gagged, but if you scream or run away then Mr. Beckman will find out and he'll have our heads. You aren't safe at your house." The other boy, Ed insisted.

"Will you just agree to sit here with us until your husbands get home?" Sam asked.

I looked at Tricia and realized they must have been desperate to protect us. Both of us nodded yes in agreement.

Sam removed our gags. "I'm very sorry for all of this." He apologized. "If you can cooperate with us we can move to a better place and you will be able to keep an eye on your houses from there without being spotted."

"Alright Sam. We will trust you for now." I told him.

They untied us and we followed them through the woods to a place that overlooked our little community.

"Sam, our husbands will be expecting us to let them into the house. They don't have a key to get in. If we aren't there to greet them, they will be upset and this plot to keep us hidden might blow up in your face." I told him.

"That is why I need to intercept them while you stay here." Sam told us. "The boys will stay with you."

"Go, do what you have to do. We'll wait here with the boys." Tricia told him as she handed him her key.

As soon as I handed my key over, Sam raced toward the docks. He wanted to meet Kurt and Ethan before they had a chance to climb on to the supply wagon for the trip home. He spotted Ethan first.

"Sam what are you doing here? Is everything alright?" He asked.

"Mrs. Bernard sent me to give you the key to your house. She's helping Mrs. Albert with one of the neighbor ladies. Her baby is coming and they won't be home when you get there. The birth is a secret so don't be saying anything on the way home. It's important. Here is Mr. Albert's key to his house too. I came right here. I didn't touch anything in your house. I'll be at the back door when you get home and I'll show you where your wives are. Remember, not a word. It would cause a big bit of trouble if it got out." Sam warned him.

"Alright Sam. I'll tell Mr. Albert and we won't let anyone

know." Ethan agreed.

"Good." Sam took off and made his way back to us.

Gus spoke to Sam when he returned. "We spotted Mr. Beckman's men knocking on Mrs. Albert's door and checking around back. Then they went to Mrs. Bernard's doors. They must believe they are shopping. They went back toward the city."

"Sam, do you know how my husband upset Mr. Beckman?" I asked him.

"No. All I heard on the street is that Mr. Beckman will lose a great deal of money if your husband doesn't agree to help him." Sam replied.

We watched the house and saw Ethan and Kurt return.

"I would go with you, but I think you should go back alone ahead of us. We will watch your backs. Stay hidden as much as possible until you are close to your homes. Explain what I told you to your husbands. Me and the boys will help any way we can. If you need me just wave out the back door. Remember to tell him I'm really sorry for what happened before." Sam was worried.

"It's alright Sam. Thank you." I told him.

Tricia and I got up and made our way home. Kurt was standing at the back door with Ethan when we arrived.

"Did you have to deliver a baby in the woods?" Kurt asked.

"Let's go inside. Lock the doors. We all have to talk." I

told him as Tricia and I went into my house.

"Kurt, there was no baby. Sam and the boys came here today about noontime. Sam said that he heard on the street that Mr. Beckman asked you to do something for him and you turned him down." I started to explain.

"That's right. He wanted me to be involved in gathering up slaves and transporting them to North Carolina. I told him I couldn't be part of that. What does that have to do with you and Tricia coming through the woods when we got home?" He asked.

"Sam said we are in big trouble. Mr. Beckman sent men to the house today to bother Tricia and me. Sam believes Mr. Beckman wants to force your hand to help him by endangering us. That is why Sam took us into the woods before those men came by. We watched the houses and saw the men banging on our doors and checking around the house. When they couldn't find us they went into the city. Sam thinks they will be back." I told him.

"How do I get hold of Sam?" Kurt asked.

"He said to wave out the back door." I told him.

He did it immediately and Sam came directly to the door with the two boys.

"Get in here and tell me what you know." Kurt ordered him.

"We get into places we really shouldn't and we overheard Mr. Beckman talking about you turning him down. He was really angry. Someone suggested that if he had leverage over you that you would do the job for him. Mr. Beckman told the man to find the leverage he needed to motivate you. The only leverage me and the boys know about is Mrs. Albert and Mrs. Bernard. So we came straight here to get them away from here and hide them until you could get home." Sam explained.

"What did the men look like who came to the house?" Kurt asked.

"There were four of them. One tall, strong looking one, he was bald. Then three others about the same size." I answered.

"It was Miller, Skaub, Dexter, and Peterman." Sam said. "They do all of Mr. Beckman's dirty work."

"I know them all." Kurt said.

"What do we do?" I was really worried.

"Well, we can't stay here." Kurt replied.

"They will find you if you hide any place in Boston." Sam told him.

"I hate running." Kurt said.

"We don't have much choice." Ethan told him.

"I guarantee you are being watched. Mr. Albert can I make a suggestion?" Sam asked.

"Sure." Kurt answered.

"Tell him you talked it over with your wife and realized you've made a mistake. Tell him the money is what you need now and you are willing to put your attitude aside. In the meantime you make arrangements to get your family out of Massachusetts. I hear lands close to the Missouri river are selling for a little over a dollar an acre. Once your family is safe, you leave too." Sam suggested.

"That is actually a good idea, except I'm not changing my mind. Mr. Beckman believes in contracts. Once I sign a contract I will be bound legally to do the job. I can't do that, but I will move my family out of here. If you help me Sam, and you and the boys want to come, we'll take you with us and give you a home." Kurt offered.

"My answer is already yes, but I'll check with the boys. What do you need me to do?" Sam asked.

"Find me someone who will sell me a covered wagon and some fine horses for a fair amount of money. Arrange a meeting for me tonight if possible. Don't give them my name and make sure none of it is stolen." Kurt told him.

"I'll get right on it." Sam left out the back door.

"What next?" Ethan asked.

"Start packing and taking things apart. We'll take as much as we can and leave the rest for our neighbors." Kurt said.

"What about being watched?" Ethan asked.

"If they think we suspect something is going on they will be parked outside all night. We laugh and smile and act as completely normal as possible." Kurt said. "Let's start with you taking Tricia home and laughing with me about nothing on the way out. Mention don't be late for work tomorrow."

"Okay, you got it." Ethan agreed.

He and Tricia left by the front door. They laughed with Kurt as they left and talked out loud. Anyone listening would have thought we were the happiest family alive without a care in the world.

As soon as they were in their own house, Tricia started packing and Ethan started taking things apart. Kurt and I were doing the same thing in our house. Sam returned a little over an hour later and came to the back door and knocked.

"It's me Mr. Albert." He whispered.

Kurt opened the door. "Any luck?"

"Yes Sir. The owner of the wagon will meet you behind the livery in an hour. This is the price he wants for his horses and the wagon. It was his wife that drove the bargain. Some women are too good at this. Sorry it's not less, but she wouldn't budge on her set price. I checked the horses. They are good, not a lame one in the bunch. I did get her to list the supplies you would need for a long trip. We can get some at the livery for the horses and food you can pick up along the way." Sam told him.

Kurt checked the list. "You did good."

An hour later Kurt left with Sam to meet the owners of the wagon and the team. He left me with Ethan. Kurt found out the people had just arrived and were staying at the hotel until they found a place to live. He offered the man a job working on the docks and explained the house rental situation.

"If you report to the dock tomorrow I will set you up with

a job. The only condition is that you don't tell anyone I bought this from you, ever. If I find out you told, I will fire you just as fast as I hired you." Kurt explained.

"You've got a deal." The man shook his hand.

"Meet me at seven in the morning. Ask anyone at the dock and they will point me out to you. Remember, your job lasts only as long as this remains between the two of us." Kurt told him.

"Anything you say Mr. Albert." The man shook Kurt's hand.

They exchanged the money and the man showed him how to hook the horses up. He instructed Kurt in a few minutes how to handle the wagon under certain conditions. Then he went over details that included anything else Kurt would need to know.

"Thank you for your help. I'll see you in the morning." Kurt told him.

Sam stepped into the driver's seat and took the reins. "Between us Mr. Albert, I'm the better driver." Sam assured him.

Kurt got up beside him. "Find a way to the back of my house without going down the main road."

"Yes Sir." Sam agreed as he steered the horses away from the livery.

Kurt was impressed. Sam was exceptionally good at driving the horses and maneuvering the wagon. After midnight we were loading the wagon. It was the middle of the night when it was finally full with only enough room left to fit all of us.

"Ethan, take everyone out of Boston. Hide the wagon and the girls and send Sam to meet me tomorrow night at the loading station in Newton. Listen to Sam. He knows about this type of journey and these horses. Let him drive the team. He is good at it." Kurt said.

"Kurt, what are you going to do?" I asked him.

"I'm reporting to work. I'll turn the keys in to Mr. Beckman's assistant after he is away from the office. I already bought a horse. It will be waiting for me at the livery. I'll meet you tomorrow night in Newton. I promise Lacey. I'll be there." He took me in his arms and kissed me. "I love you Lacey. I promise. I'll be there." Then he picked me up and put me in the back of the wagon next to Tricia and the boys.

"Don't worry Mr. Albert." Sam smiled.

"Go now Sam. Instruct Ethan as you go. That way he can drive the team if you need to rest." Kurt told him.

Sam pulled away as we waved to Kurt. He went back into the house to rest. In the morning he came out to the supply wagon alone.

"Where's Athan?" The driver asked.

"He was too sick this morning. I'm sure he will be fine tomorrow. Let's go." Kurt said.

The driver took all the men to work. Kurt hired the new

man and had him fill out all the necessary paper work. Then he put him to work. After lunch he watched Mr. Beckman leave the dock. He quickly put his assistant in charge.

"Trevor, take over until I return. I have some important details to straighten out." Kurt told him.

"Yes Sir." Trevor took over just like he had done a number of times before.

Kurt walked to the office and handed an envelope to Mr. Beckman's assistant. "This is for Mr. Beckman's eyes only."

"Certainly Mr. Albert, but he won't be back until four o'clock." The assistant told him.

"Not a problem. The deadline is next week." Kurt said as he watched the assistant put the envelope on Mr. Beckman's desk. Then he left and went directly to the livery to pick up his horse. He was careful not to take any of the main roads out of Boston.

Sam was waiting at the loading station when Kurt rode up on his horse. "It's nice to see you again, Mr. Albert."

Kurt reached down and grabbed Sam by the arm and pulled him up behind him on the horse. "Show me where to find the others."

Sam took him out of town to a large farm. "Ethan worked out a deal with the owner, food and shelter for a night at a price. No one will find us here."

The farmer, Mr. Bernard and his wife were really friendly. They thought Ethan and Tricia might be distant relatives because of their last name. They welcomed Kurt and Sam to supper. The next morning they gave us extra eggs and biscuits for the journey ahead and blessed our way.

Sam took over driving the team. We headed for the Missouri river and our future. When we stopped for the night, Sam helped Kurt set up the campsite while Ethan took Tricia and me for a private walk to take care of business.

We ate well together and talked.

"What did you put in the envelope?" Ethan asked.

"The keys to our houses and a note that the furniture we left behind could go to the new owners. I also thanked him for his kindness in offering me a job and explained that we had decided to move to Maine together." Kurt explained. "I told him I had a good job offer that included being the Captain of a fishing vessel and I had to take the job immediately."

Tricia and I slept in the wagon together and our husbands slept out in the open with the boys.

"I sure do envy you Mr. Albert and Mr. Bernard; your wives are very pretty ladies and very nice." Sam said. "Me and the boys appreciate you taking us in like this. We haven't had a home or family besides ourselves in years."

"You just keep a respectful attitude and we will all get along just fine." Ethan told them. "I'm warning you now, Tricia and Lacey have intentions of teaching you all how to read among other things."

"What other things?" Gus asked.

"Proper manners and how to stay cleaner." Kurt smiled.

"You mean a bath? No woman is making me take a bath." Ed objected.

Kurt laughed. "Don't get too big for your britches. If my wife demands it, you will do it if you're going to be part of this family."

Ed pulled the blanket over his head and went to sleep mumbling his complaints to himself.

Chapter Nine

Just before we got into Missouri territory we had a family discussion to set up the dynamics of our little family unit.

"Boys, come sit down." Kurt called them over toward himself and Ethan.

"What is it Mr. Albert?" Sam asked.

"Lacey and I have discussed how our family will look with you boys as part of it and we've come to some decisions. Lacey is twenty-one now and I'm twenty-eight. We need to know your ages." Kurt told him.

"I'm just about seventeen, Ed is fifteen and his brother Gus is thirteen." Sam answered.

"We'll there is no way either Lacey or Tricia can be passed off as your mothers so we are going to make them your aunts. From now on you will refer to me as Uncle Kurt and call my wife Aunt Lacey. You will call Mr. Bernard Uncle Athan when people outside the family are present, but we know he is Uncle Ethan. Refer to his wife as Aunt Tricia. You will be respectful at all times. I'm much bigger than you and if you disrespect your aunts you will answer to me and your Uncle Ethan. Do you understand?" Kurt warned them.

"Yes Sir." They all said simultaneously.

"From now on your last names are Albert. You will be known as Sam Albert, Ed Albert and Gus Albert. It will make things a whole lot easier for all of us. Any objections?" Kurt asked.

"We made up our last names a long time ago to keep us out of trouble. We changed them on a regular basis anyway, so Albert is just as good as any we've had." Gus explained.

We were all surprised by that statement.

"You boys are brothers now. If anyone asks who your parents' names were, what will you tell them?" Kurt asked.

"We will tell them our parents died a tragic death and we don't discuss it with anyone because it is too painful for us." Sam insisted.

The other boys agreed.

"Alright then. The plan is to buy enough land to build two houses on. You boys will be doing a lot of labor. This life won't be easy, but you will be well fed and provided for. If you want to leave us and move out on your own when you are each eighteen, you can do that. If you get into trouble I will treat you like I would my own sons. Any time you don't want me as the father figure in your life, move on as far away as possible because if you choose to live close, the law is clear that I am responsible for you. You will treat every female with respect and consideration. You will speak respectfully to adults and regard young children as in need of protection. Our households believe in Father God, Jesus his son who died for our sins and is our Savior and Lord and the Holy Spirit. You will not take the name of the Lord in vain in our homes. You will join us when we bless our meals before you eat. You will not play the heathen or the atheist in our homes, church or if you are so blessed, school. Is that understood and accepted?" Kurt asked.

"Yes Sir." They agreed.

"When you are old enough to leave our home it is our hope that you will be the best kind of men that anyone would be proud to know. One more thing; all of us here care about all of you. We want this to work out for all of you. Our wives have grown to love all of you and Ethan and I certainly want you as a real part of our families." Kurt said.

Everyone got up from the meeting and Tricia and I made sure to hug each of the boys. They immediately started referring to us as their uncles and aunts.

Kurt took Sam aside. "You're older than the other boys, so when we are alone you call me Kurt and you can refer to my wife as Lacey, but when anyone else is around including Gus and Ed, it is Uncle Kurt and Aunt Lacey."

"I'll be sure to do it your way." Sam agreed.

A week later we arrived in Missouri. Kurt checked the local newspaper and determined the best spot to buy land was along the Missouri riverfront. Lots were selling for one hundred and thirty dollars. We still had gold coin from Prentice which we had tucked away for our future. We managed to get ourselves to the center of Lohman's Landing. It was a city that bordered the Missouri River. Kurt and Ethan quickly found out where to go to purchase the land. They bought four lots that were joined together along the water front; two in Athan Bernard's name and two in Curtis Albert's name. As soon as the properties were registered to us we continued on to the hardware store to arrange for building supplies and materials.

"Come back with an empty wagon Mr. Albert and we will load you up." The storekeeper told my husband as they shook on the deal.

We continued to our land and the boys helped us unload the wagon. Kurt and Ethan took it back into Lohman's Landing and got it loaded. They were back to the property a little over an hour later. Kurt set the boys to digging for an outhouse first and far enough away from where the main house would be. Sam, Ethan, and Kurt set up a foundation line and started to dig for the main supports of the house. They leveled out the land for our first house. Tricia and I organized the supplies we had from the wagon and kept the men supplied with water and food while they worked. They never stopped. As soon as they were finished with one thing Ethan directed each of them on to the next. I was so glad my brother was a master builder and had decided that Kurt and I needed the first house with the boys. It took us a month of constant work to finish the first house with a barn. As soon as we were done we started Ethan and Tricia's house. It was another two months before their house and barn were completed. Each day we thanked God and asked him to bless Prentice Sheffield for the great generosity he had shown us.

Our neighbors started to appear around us. Each took the time to admire our homes and the workmanship that went into them. They were standing in line wanting to hire Ethan and his building crew. Once more we had fallen into the grace of God. Ethan and Kurt formed their own successful building company with the three boys working alongside.

At supper one evening as I was serving the men of my family I voiced a concern.

"Kurt, I know you need the boys to work alongside you and Ethan. I'm very proud of the hard work they do, but I have a request." I said.

"What request?" He asked.

"I would like to teach the boys how to read better. I know they have been busy nearly every day, but there has to be some time in the day for learning." I told him.

"Lacey, what they do with their hands is learning. Sam is nearly as good a carpenter as I am. Gus is measuring things every day. He and Ed are good with angles and measurements. Their practical math skills are being tested every day. They read designs." Kurt said.

"I know that they understand drawings and graphs. I know they work hard and have vision for what is ahead, but Kurt if they don't learn how to read better they will never enjoy God's word like you and I do. They won't know how to go over a legal contract. They need to know how to read better and write better or someone else will be directing their paths when they are older. Please give me an hour a day with each of them to teach them to read and write better." I asked him.

Kurt looked at the boys who were apparently not enthusiastic about my request. "Alright, one hour a day."

We heard the moans from the table.

"You will respect my wishes and do your best for my wife. Anyone who does not do his best will not work with me and instead of one hour you might be stuck here all day reading. I will remind you there is no pay unless you work." Kurt said sternly.

"Yes Sir." They answered him reluctantly.

I smiled at my success. "What hour may I have them?"

"Seven to eight in the morning." He said.

"I need to know how well they read first. I'll take Gus tomorrow morning and work with him this first week alone. Then next week Ed will stay behind with us, and the third week Sam will join us for the hour." I told Kurt.

"As you wish." Kurt agreed.

Later that night we climbed into bed together.

"I appreciated you backing me up with the boys tonight." I told him as I climbed under the covers.

"Lacey, do you know why I designed this house with all the boy's rooms on the other side of the dining room?" He asked me as he took off his shirt.

"Yes, so that we could have privacy upstairs and a section of the house for ourselves and a family of our own someday." I told him.

"Exactly." He said as he climbed into bed beside me. "And part of that privacy includes that you do not talk about the boys every night. Lately you have been doing that like you were their mother."

"Are you jealous?" I asked him.

"Yes, very." He admitted as he put his arm under my neck and drew me closer. "Not another word about them or your day or Tricia or anything that will distract us from this time together. All I want when we enter this part of the house is us. I want you all to myself from now on. I need you Lacey. I love you."

It didn't take him very long to convince me that shutting the world out of this section of our home was a very good idea.

In the middle of the night I got on my robe and went downstairs to get a drink of water. I was surprised when I caught Sam coming into the house.

"Sam, what were you doing outside?" I startled him as I asked him.

"I couldn't sleep so I went for a walk in the night air." He said. "Goodnight Lacey."

"Goodnight Sam." I wanted to believe he was telling the truth but I knew I shouldn't keep this a secret from Kurt.

The next morning Gus stayed behind after the others left. I opened my bible and asked him to read one of the Psalms. He stumbled on some words and didn't know others. I helped him to read for an hour making note of the words he didn't know.

"Gus, I'm going to make you a spelling list of the words you don't know. Then tomorrow you can work on spelling them and memorizing them. Then we will try again." I told him.

"Yes Aunt Lacey." He agreed.

"Go off now and join the others." I told him. "Sam left the horse saddled for you. Be careful."

"I will." He said as he left.

That evening the boys were very quiet at supper and so was Kurt. That evening Kurt was very attentive to me again. Once again I got up after he had fallen asleep and went down into the kitchen to get a drink. Once again I caught Sam coming into the house.

"Sam, sit down." I insisted.

"It's very late Lacey. I'm just starting to feel like I can sleep again. Can this wait till morning?" He tried to avoid me.

"No it cannot." I insisted. "Please sit."

He shook his head knowing he was about to be in trouble. He sat down on the couch.

"What is going on with you? What is going on with all of you? Tonight at supper you all looked like you were holding some kind of secret from me. This is the second night you've been caught coming in the house. Sam, talk to me. Is it a girl or are you doing something that could get you into trouble with the law?" I asked him.

"Lacey, you should be asking Kurt about this." He whined.

"Does Kurt know you've been sneaking out?" I asked him.

"I haven't been sneaking." Sam answered.

"If I mention it to him will he know why you are out walking around late at night?" I asked him.

"He might have a pretty good idea." Sam said.

"Spill it." I insisted.

"This isn't the type of thing I should be sharing with you. Can we just leave it the way it is? I'm seventeen and soon to be eighteen. I haven't hurt anyone. This is man stuff." He said.

"Wait here." I went upstairs to wake up Kurt.

"What is it Lacey?" He whispered as I shook him to wake him up.

"This is the second night Sam has come home in the middle of the night. I asked him why he was out and he said he couldn't sleep so he went for a walk." I explained.

"Yes, so?" He asked.

"Well Kurt, I pressed the issue and he said he can't discuss it with me and that it is men stuff. What men stuff? Go find out what he has been up to." I demanded.

Kurt got up. "Wait here." Then he walked to the edge of the staircase and called down to Sam. "Sam, go to bed!"

"Yes Sir." Sam got right up and went to his room.

"Why didn't you go see what the problem is?" I asked him

as he came back into the bedroom.

"Because it is late and I'm tired. Go to sleep Lacey." He climbed into bed. He was asleep in seconds.

I was aggravated with him and decided to take the matter into my own hands. The next morning I put breakfast on the table before all of my family came to the table. We sat down and Kurt held his hands out like he had done every morning expecting me and Ed to take his hand for the blessing of the meal. I refused my hand.

"Lacey, is there a problem?" He asked me.

"Yes. Before you all eat I want to say something." I insisted.

Everyone pulled back their hands.

"Go ahead Lacey." Kurt said.

"I know that something is going on with all of you and I want to know what it is." I insisted.

Ed and Gus immediately put their heads down in guilt and I saw Kurt look at Sam. Sam shook his head no.

"What is going on?" I demanded an answer.

"Lacey, you and I can talk about this after breakfast. Let the boys eat." Kurt said.

"Very well. All of you enjoy your breakfast." I reached for Kurt's hand for the blessing.

Everyone held hands and Kurt blessed the meal. Then

they all started to eat. I moved my chair back and left the table and went upstairs without saying anything. All the boys continued to eat and watch me walk up the stairs. Kurt wasn't motivated to follow me. He had already stated that he would talk to me after breakfast and he wasn't about to change his mind.

"You boys clean off your spots after you are done then wait outside until I finish discussing this with your aunt." He moved his chair back and wiped his mouth with the napkin. Then he went upstairs to talk to me. He entered our bedroom. "Alright Lacey, let's talk."

"I'm waiting." I sat on the bed and stared at him.

"We have a job working in town on the hotel. There is a little distraction across the street that seems to have the boys on edge." He started to explain.

"What kind of a distraction?" I asked him.

"Women." He answered.

"I don't understand. Why would women be so distracting to the boys? They have seen women before."

"These particular women make their living by getting the attention of men. There is a men's club in the city." He explained.

"Oh, so that is what they are calling it now?" I stood up from the bed. "That explains a lot. It's not just the boys who have been affected by these women is it? Is Ethan being as distracted as you are too?"

"I haven't done anything wrong." He insisted.

"Really? Then why haven't you addressed the issue of Sam going out and staying out at night?" I asked him.

"Sam got a job on the side at night. I told him I couldn't spare him during the day so he goes out at night and works." He explained.

"Doing what? Who can he work for so late at night?" I asked him.

"He is building some items inside the men's club. A few of the women hired him." Kurt said.

"And you let him?" I was upset by the information.

"He is nearly eighteen. He's been living on the streets for years. I'm not his father. He is more independent than the other two boys and he is nearly an adult. He took the job and worked out the hours so that he wouldn't take the man hours away from the projects Ethan and I have." Kurt explained.

"And how are they paying him?" I shouted at Kurt.

"Why don't you ask him?" Kurt shouted back.

"Fine, I will." I went to push past him and he grabbed me by the arm.

"Sit down!" Kurt yelled at me. "Sam is a man, not a boy and you are not his mother. You are barely four years older than he is. He has been well mannered and helpful around here. He gives himself completely to helping this household. You should respect him enough to let him make his own way in life. We offered him a home and he is an asset to this family.

Don't think for one minute that you are more important than you are. He doesn't owe you an explanation. He has already cleared this with me."

"It is apparent Mr. Albert that you think very little of me. Since we got here you have been a dictator in this house. I have become your cook and your housekeeper. I am only your wife by your great permission or your recent desire which is probably motivated by this distraction you just told me about. You see me as less than yourself and you regard me that way. I have become of little importance to you. Why else would you speak to me in such a way? We agreed that the boys would be part of this family. We would be responsible for them. Yes, I feel like their mother because I love them. I don't want my sons getting into trouble with wayward women. I am concerned for Sam. I have a perfect right to talk to him. So what if I am barely four years older than him. I am your wife and he is part of our family. If you want to disregard my concerns go right ahead, but I will address Sam. I will ask him questions. We will have a conversation about this, because I care about him. Now don't think for one minute that I will put up with the lack of kindness you have shown me. You are my husband, but you don't own me and you are not the boss of my heart. You cannot command it away from loving these boys and acting on that love." I declared.

"Lacey, leave him be." Kurt said sternly.

"Go to work. Our conversation is over." I told him.

"I'll leave Ed and Gus with you for lessons." He said as he reached for the doorknob.

"No, not today. I have plans." I told him.

"What plans?" He asked.

"I'm visiting Tricia." I told him.

"Don't start trouble Lacey." He warned me.

"I've got nothing more to say to you today Mr. Albert." I told him.

He left the room and joined the boys outside. He left with all of them. I went downstairs and finished my breakfast. Then I washed the dishes. After that I put on my shawl. I walked to Tricia's house and explained about the men's club.

"Tricia, I think we need to take a ride into the city and find out for ourselves how much of a distraction these women are to our husbands." I suggested.

"I think you're right. Ethan hadn't mentioned them, but he hasn't been himself lately either." She told me.

We hooked up her carriage with her horse and rode into the city. We stopped at the livery and let the owner take care of the horse and carriage while we walked toward our husbands' job site. We found a good vantage point to watch the men while they worked outside the hotel. We were inside a dress shop across the street watching from the window as we went through some items slowly. We both saw the young ladies approach our husbands and flirt with them as they worked. Ethan and Kurt smiled and laughed as the ladies spoke with them, but they never stopped working. Sam was in on the flirting too as Ed and Gus looked on.

"Time to make our presence known." I told Tricia.

"Not without some store bought items in our hands." Tricia said.

"I'm not using any excuses. I want them to know I was spying. Are you coming?" I asked her.

Tricia watched as another woman approached her husband. "Yes I am."

We walked out of the dress shop and directly across the street to the hotel. Gus and Ed were the first ones who saw us coming.

"Hello Aunt Lacey and Aunt Tricia." They yelled and waved.

Sam looked up in our direction and quickly grabbed his tools and went inside the hotel. He waved to us as he left.

Ethan looked at Tricia and whispered to Kurt. "I'm in trouble."

"This is Lacey's doing." Kurt whispered back.

I greeted the ladies who were hanging around our husbands. "Hello Ladies." I said cheerfully.

They each responded in kind.

Then one of them named Lia addressed me. "So you are the aunts to Gus and Ed?"

"Actually, we are aunts to Sam too." I answered her.

"You're a little young to be Sam's aunts, aren't you?" Lia asked.

"No." I answered.

"So what relation are you to Ethan and Kurt?" She asked me as the other four ladies looked on.

"We are married to them." Tricia answered.

"Really? We had no idea they were married." Lia told us. "They aren't wearing wedding rings and they never mentioned you two."

I looked at Kurt's hand and Tricia looked at Ethan's. We were surprised that their wedding rings were gone. Kurt and Ethan realized our surprise even though we didn't show it to the ladies.

"Well, now you know." I said to Lia.

"I guess we do." Then she turned to the other girls. "Let's get back to work ladies, these men have commitments already."

Tricia walked over to Ethan and whispered in his ear. "You are in so much trouble when you get home."

"Tricia, I can explain." He whispered back.

"No Ethan, you can't." She walked away and I walked away with her.

"At least Lacey didn't threaten you." Ethan said to Kurt.

"That means nothing." Kurt said. "Get back to work."

Everyone showed up at the house just before the sun went down. The boys and Kurt rushed to wash up. I set out everyone's dish and drink. Then I sat in my seat. Kurt reached for my hand and Ed's and everyone bowed their heads while he said grace.

We all started eating at the same time. Kurt and Sam started choking on their meal and drinking down their entire glass of water. I figured it was the red pepper I had saturated their meals with. Ed, Gus and I enjoyed our meals without an incident.

Kurt and Sam left the table and ran to get more water.

"She's trying to kill us." Sam struggled to whisper the words to Kurt.

Kurt just nodded yes to him as he desperately drank more water.

Ed and Gus didn't say a word, but they tried hard not to laugh. I just continued to enjoy my meal. Kurt reached in front of me and grabbed my plate and exchanged it for Sam's.

Sam sat down barely able to whisper. "Thank you."

Kurt pulled me from my chair as the boys watched. He picked me up in his arms and carried me upstairs to our bedroom.

"This family is interesting." Gus said.

"Mind your business and eat." Sam struggled to say.

Kurt put me on the bed. He had to clear his throat five times in order to be able to speak to me. The tears of the pain he had suffered made his eyes glassy. I just waited on the bed with my arms folded.

"Lacey, that was cruel." He said.

"Was it?"

"Look, I understand that you are upset about me not wearing my wedding band, but I can explain that. Ethan and I are sawing and hammering all day. We have to carry boards full of nails. If our wedding rings get caught on something we could lose our fingers or damage the rings. It is just safer to keep them tucked away in our pockets." He explained.

"Okay." I got up to leave the room.

"Where are you going?" He asked me.

"You explained so we are done talking aren't we?" I reached for the doorknob.

"No, we aren't done. Why did you serve that dish to Sam?" He asked me.

"I thought he should get of taste of the fires of Hell, just like you." I said like it was no big deal.

"Fires of Hell? Why?" He asked.

"I watched him flirting with those ladies just like you and Ethan. I thought it would be enlightening for the both of you. I am sure Ethan is sampling the fires of Hell too tonight." I told him.

"So you and Tricia came up with this to teach us a lesson?"

"Among other things." I told him.

"What other things?" He asked.

There was a knock on our bedroom door. Kurt opened it to Sam. "What is it?"

"I really need to talk to you." Sam said.

"Now?" Kurt asked.

"Oh yeah." Sam said.

"Lacey don't leave this room. We are not finished." Kurt left the room and followed Sam.

Sam brought Kurt into his room. He opened his bureau drawer and pulled out all his underwear. "Lacey cut holes in all my britches. There isn't a one that I can wear now. Why is she so angry with me? What's going on?"

"She saw you flirting with those ladies today and she wants to give you a taste of the fires of Hell." Kurt told him.

"Kurt, you have to put a stop to this." He begged him.

"I'll talk to her. Are you working tonight?" Kurt asked him.

"Yes, I have one more door to fix for Lia." He said.

"Sam, how are they paying you for your work?" Kurt asked.

"What do you mean?" Sam asked.

"You know what I mean." Kurt said.

"No Kurt, it's not like that. I want a nice girl like Lacey in my life. I don't want those women. They pay me in cash. I have my eye on a girl from the church. This is just work. I just flirt with the girls to drum up more business." Sam told him.

"Good to know. I'll tell Lacey you won't be flirting with the ladies again." Kurt said.

"Yes, let her know I got the point and I won't be doing that anymore. Let her know after tonight I won't be working for them either. I need Lacey on my side. She's dangerous when she is angry." Sam said.

Kurt left Sam and returned to our bedroom. He went to his bureau and pulled out his britches and found every one of them had holes cut out of them. "Lacey, was this really necessary?"

"This way you don't have to take the time to take them off. You can get right down to business with Lia and her friends." I said casually.

"This is ridiculous. I'm married to you. I love you. Ethan loves Tricia." He said.

"Really? Then why didn't those ladies know you were married? Why didn't you mention to them that you had a wife?" I asked him.

"The job is never ending. The ladies are funny. They amuse us. They bring us drinks during the day and sandwiches at lunch time. We appreciated the provision. They didn't ask and we didn't offer the information. Ed, Gus and Sam got a nice lunch out of the deal just like Ethan and me. Ethan loves Tricia. I love you. We know we are married. Nothing happened except some friendly conversation and a few nice lunches." He explained.

"Okay." I grabbed the doorknob to leave.

Kurt stopped me again. He put his arms around me. "Lacey, I was wrong. I should have told them that I was married to you. I should have been more interested in what Sam was doing. He assured me that he got your point. He has one more door to fix for Lia tonight and he is done with the girls. He was only flirting to drum up more business with them, but he thought better of it. He won't be working for them after this. They paid him money, not favors. Sam is interested in a nice girl from church. He said he wants a nice girl like you. He wanted you to know that he will be staying away from the ladies after he finishes the last job tonight."

"That's good to know." I said.

"Lacey honey, please let's not fight anymore. I thought about what you said today and you were right. I have been acting badly toward you. I've been so busy building things with Ethan and managing the business and the boys that I started managing you too. We haven't been married very long and we've been through so much in such a short time that I lost sight of us. I don't want to be the beast in charge. I really want to love my wife and not take her for granted. Please forgive me Lacey. Can we stop all this fighting and get back to loving each other?" He asked.

"Are you still hungry?" I asked him.

"Starving." He answered.

"Come downstairs and I'll make us both something that we can eat." I told him.

He kissed me first and we went downstairs together.

Sam was coming out of his room. "Aunt Lacey, I'm sorry I upset you." He apologized.

"Apology accepted Sam." I told him.

He kissed me on the cheek. "I'll be home in a few hours."

"Stay safe." I told him and watched him leave. Then I made Kurt and me something to eat.

Ed and Gus did their spelling work while Kurt and I finished eating. A few hours later Sam came home and everyone went to bed at the same time.

Ethan met all of them in the morning. "I see you survived the fires of Hell."

"Yes, but Sam and I had to wear yesterday's britches today. We are stopping by the General Store today to pick up a new supply. Lacey cut holes in all of them to make a point." Kurt told him.

Ethan laughed. "You need new britches and I need new shirts. Tricia sewed all my sleeves shut. She said it was so my hands wouldn't be free to touch other women."

Kurt and Sam laughed along with Ed and Gus.

Then Sam turned to Gus and Ed. "Remember to never upset a woman."

Chapter Ten

A year went by and business was very good. We were all settled into our lives and I thought it was about time I wrote to Prentice Sheffield. I mailed the letter which arrived at his manor more than six weeks later. Milton brought it to him.

"Thank you Milton." He opened it and read it.

Dear Prentice,

With your help we escaped and were married. Kurt and I were married at sea by the Captain, along side Ethan and Tricia. We boarded a vessel for Boston and did as you advised so that we could start new lives.

We thought we were blessed when Kurt and Ethan were offered jobs before we left the ship, but we were mistaken. Slave trade had crept in and when Kurt refused to be part of it, once again we were at risk. We had to flee Boston and now we live in middle America.

We've sort of adopted three boys. They are all teenagers and very nice young men. Kurt and Ethan are carpenters and very well respected in this area. Our houses are built near the Missouri river. Kurt needs to be near water. We love our new home and our neighbors are very nice.

I wanted to write to you and thank you for all your help and for the generosity you have shown us. We have a good life because of it. I have enclosed our address and new names if you wish to write back. I know I can trust you with this information. I would like nothing more than to see you again. All of us miss you greatly. I wanted you to know that we are safe. We can never repay your great kindness to us. I pray for you often Prentice. I shall never forget you.

Love Always,

    Lacey

Prentice was excited to sit down and write back to me. He gave Milton the letter and asked him to arrange for it to go out on the next ship. Milton sent it with one of the servants, giving her instructions not to let the letter out of her sight until it was hand delivered to the man in charge of collecting mail on the island. She ran into town and directly to Joseph Carlyle.

"You've done well Matilda." He slipped her a few coins. "Wait while I examine this one too."

She waited in the street for him as he went into his father's office and opened the letter carefully.

Dearest Lacey,

I was thrilled to receive your letter and find that you were doing so well in America. That is a great undertaking to adopt three young boys into your family. I would have thought by now I would have heard news of you and Kurt having a baby or at least Ethan and Tricia.

Joseph was very upset to discover you had left the area successfully. He searched for months trying to discover your whereabouts. He was to return to England soon after your departure, but he has yet to give up on finding you. I believe his obsession is mentally unhealthy to him. The kind man we once knew no longer seems to exist. He treats even his parents with distain. You were very fortunate to have escaped a future with him.

Life on the island is not as peaceful as we would like. We too have been invaded by slave traders. Before we were able to run them off the island some of the nicest families here have lost sons and daughters to them. The Carlyle family and myself have organized a Shipmaster to patrol the island and run off those who wish to come here to cause harm. We are united with businesses in the area to protect the citizens of the island from such men.

Please keep in touch. I do miss the cheerful sound of your voices in the manor. It has been lonely at times. Keep well and give my love to the others.

Affectionately yours,

Prentice Sheffield

Joseph folded the letter and sealed it carefully. He wrote the address down and stuffed it into his pocket. Then he went outside to Matilda and handed it back to her.

"Bring it to be mailed. Remember, as long as you keep this between us you will be paid for your service." Joseph told her.

"Yes Sir, Mr. Carlyle." She left and ran to turn the letter over to the man in charge of the outgoing mail.

Joseph made immediate arrangements to travel to England. He informed his parents that he would be leaving the island in three days. They were not unhappy about his departure. Once in England he made arrangements to board a ship for America. He brought every document he could gather up that proved that Ethan Dopolis was a wanted criminal. He took the ship to Boston and then arranged to travel to Missouri.

By now Lohman's Landing had been renamed Jefferson City. Joseph checked out the city and made inquiries about the Albert family. He found that Ethan and Kurt owned a very successful business under new names. He checked with the Sheriff and explained the situation. He wanted the Sheriff to arrest Ethan.

"I'm sorry Mr. Carlyle, but it is your word against his. His legal name is Athan Bernard, not Ethan Dopolis. I have no proof that they are the same person. Mr. Bernard is very well known in this part of the country. He has an impeccable reputation and no one here knows who you are. I will not support your accusations by bothering my friend Athan Bernard. Athan has not broken any laws here. Save yourself a problem with the people around here and drop this. This is not England. You have no power here to manipulate the law. This is America." The Sheriff told him.

"You are absolutely right Sheriff. It is very possible they are not the same person and my information is wrong. I will not cause any more problems for Mr. Bernard. Please keep this between us. I do not wish to start off in this community on the wrong footing with someone you apparently respect. I apologize for troubling you." Joseph said.

"Alright Mr. Carlyle. You have a good day Sir." The Sheriff opened his door and Joseph left.

Joseph spent the next month studying my family. He knew each of our schedules and the dynamics of the family. He wanted to arrange for a time to approach me without Kurt or Ethan around.

One morning as Kurt was having breakfast with us before work someone knocked on our door. Kurt got up and opened the door.

"May I help you?" He asked the man standing in front of him wearing a business suit.

"Good morning Mr. Albert. My name is Thadeus Conner. I have been sent by my employer to seek out builders in this area and make them aware that we are accepting bids on this project for Jefferson City. I would like to drop off the specifications for this project and invite you to bid on the job." He explained as he stood at the door.

"I appreciate the offer Mr. Conner, but my partner and I are already booked until the middle of next year. We won't have time to get involved with your project." Kurt told him.

"You and Mr. Bernard have a very good reputation. This project will not be starting immediately. Would you consider looking over the design and writing up a bid? It could prove quite profitable for you. My employer is willing to pay for quality work." He tried to hand Kurt the plans.

"Thank you again, but no." Kurt said.

"Are you sure Mr. Albert?" He asked again.

"Quite sure. Good day Mr. Conner." Kurt shut the door and returned to the breakfast table.

"What was that all about?" I asked him when he sat down.

"I was praying this morning and I felt like the good Lord warned me about that man at the door. There is something not right about him and the deal he offered." Kurt explained.

"You know best." I smiled.

Mr. Conner returned to Joseph to tell him that the bait was refused. Joseph wasn't happy that his plan hadn't worked. He paid the man for his services and insisted that he leave the city as soon as possible. Joseph paid for his silence and his departure.

The more Joseph checked around the more he realized that his plans to disrupt our lives would be nearly impossible. We were well established in the community and we had no enemies. He decided he couldn't wait any longer. He wanted me to know that he was nearby and he still wanted me in his life. He waited until Kurt and the boys left for work. He watched Kurt kiss me goodbye at the door. Then he waited another half hour to make sure no one was coming back.

I went outside to check the garden for tomatoes. I was gathering them up on my knees and I saw the shadow of someone cross between me and the sun. When I looked up Joseph was standing in front of me.

"Hello Lacey." He smiled down at me.

I was shocked and frightened at the sight of him. I started to try to get to my feet and he got down on his knees in front of me and grabbed my arms.

"No need to get up. I think we should have our conversation right here, just like this." He insisted.

"Let go of me Joseph! I have nothing to say to you." I tried to pull free from his grip.

"Do you honestly believe that you have any hope of getting free of me?" He taunted me.

I heard Sam riding back toward the yard and I screamed for him. "Sam! Help me!"

Joseph quickly stood to his feet as Sam pulled his horse up in front of us and dismounted. Sam went directly to me and helped me off the ground.

"What is going on here? Who are you?" Sam demanded.

"I'm an old friend of Lacey's." He said and extended his hand to shake Sam's.

"He is no friend. Take me into the house Sam and away from him." I said.

"Mister, you'd better leave. You're not welcome here." Sam told him as he walked me to the front door.

"I'll be around Lacey. We haven't finished our discussion." Joseph said as he got on his horse. Then he left the property.

Sam took me inside and locked the door. "He's gone now."

I started crying immediately and Sam held on to me.

"I won't leave you." He promised.

Kurt noticed it was taking a very long time for Sam to return with the tools he sent him for. He sent Gus to go find out what the problem was. Gus showed up at the house about an hour later and came in to find Sam consoling me on the couch.

"Gus, go get Kurt. Tell him Lacey needs him." Sam told him.

Gus turned around and left immediately. About twenty minutes later Kurt came into the house.

I ran into his arms as soon as he came through the front door.

"What is going on? What happened?" He asked me.

"Joseph Carlyle was here." I told him.

"He was standing over Lacey when I got here. I told him to leave and I took her inside the house. She has been too upset for me to return to you. I couldn't leave her alone." Sam explained.

"Sam, return to work. Give me an hour and then you send Gus back here." Kurt told him.

"Yes Sir." Sam left the house and collected the tools he had originally come for. Then he headed back to work.

Kurt sat with me on the couch. He kept his arm around me. "Lacey, tell me what happened."

"I was in the garden on my knees gathering up some of the tomatoes. I noticed a shadow over me so I looked up and Joseph Carlyle was standing over me. I went to get up but he got down on his knees in front of me and grabbed my arms. He wouldn't let go of me. He just held me there in front of him. He told me that unless he wanted to let me up there was no way I was going to get away from him. That's when I heard Sam coming so I screamed for him. Joseph was standing when Sam got to me. Sam told him to leave and took me into the house. Kurt, Joseph said that he planned on talking to me again. I know he is going to bother us and cause trouble for Ethan."

"I'm going to go see the Sheriff about him. Lacey, everyone in this town knows us as the Alberts and the Bernards and that is just the way it is going to stay. I am going to file a complaint against him in town as if he was a stranger to us and just showed up to threaten my wife." Kurt said.

"The Sheriff will have questions about all of us if you claim he is a stranger." I worried.

"Then I'll tell him that you knew him years ago and he proposed to you, but you were already married to me. I'll tell him the man is crazy and has been searching for you and trying to make trouble for your family. We stick to our new legal names. I'll talk to Ethan and Tricia and warn them. Then I'll have Sam do what he does best and check around the city to see what Joseph is up to." He said.

Kurt and I talked until Gus got back home.

"Gus, you stick to Lacey like glue. Don't let her out of your sight." Kurt said.

"Yes Sir." Gus agreed. He was a teenage boy, but he had developed some muscles and he was taller than me.

Kurt kissed me goodbye. "I'll take care of this Lacey. He's not going to bother you."

Gus helped me to collect vegetables from the garden. He made himself useful to me the rest of the day. I got him to repair a few things for me while he was home.

Kurt spoke with Ethan first. During lunch time Ethan took a ride home to Tricia and warned her about what was going on. Tricia loaded her gun. She wasn't about to let Joseph intimidate her. Then Kurt took a ride to the Sheriff's office.

"Jebb, I need to talk to you about something." Kurt said as he entered the office.

"You sound serious. Have a seat. How can I help you?" Jebb asked.

"This morning a man by the name of Joseph Carlyle came on to my property and threatened my wife. I want you to lock him up." Kurt said.

"Was he drunk?" Jebb asked.

"No." Kurt answered.

"Well tell me the details first." Jebb said.

"Years ago this guy wanted to marry my wife. She turned him down and married me instead. Since then he has been stalking her and making wild accusations about our family. We came here to get away from him and we have no idea how he found us. He crossed the line this morning. Lacey was in the garden and he grabbed her. She was home alone. She tried to get away from him and he wouldn't let go of her. I sent Sam back to our house to get some tools and he rescued my wife. My wife is upset and I'm upset. I want him to stay away from my wife. I don't want trouble. I just want him to stay away from Lacey and my family." Kurt explained.

"He got into town over a month ago. He came here with papers that claimed that Athan was really Ethan Dopolis, a man wanted in England for stealing. I sent him on his way. He asked me to forget the matter and not mention it to Athan. So I gave him the benefit and didn't say anything. You and your family have a good name in Jefferson City. I'll make sure to go have a talk with Mr. Carlyle. I'll throw him in jail overnight to make my point. If he bothers you or your family again after that then come and see me. Maybe one night in jail will cause him to rethink his plans to bother your wife. Keep your head Kurt. Don't let him bait you." Jebb warned as he grabbed his handcuffs and put his gun on.

"Thanks Jebb." Kurt said as he left.

Jebb did just what he said he would. He found Joseph Carlyle in the Men's Club and handcuffed him. Then he brought him back to jail and put him in a cell.

"I don't like trouble in this city. This twenty-four hour hold is a warning to you. You leave Mrs. Albert alone and stay away from her family and Mr. Bernard's family. They are good people and you are a stranger to me. I will take their word over yours any day of the week. If you bother them again your stay in jail will be much longer." Jebb threatened.

Joseph was very upset by his situation. "They have pulled the wool over your eyes Sheriff! They are the guilty party, not me!"

"Mr. Carlyle your attitude will get you another day in jail. Do you want that?" Jebb threatened.

"No Sir, I don't." He was exasperated at the injustice he felt.

"Then calm yourself and face the facts. You touched another man's wife. You are fortunate Mr. Albert agreed to this warning and didn't press the issue. Next time he won't be so merciful and neither will I." Jebb walked away from the locked cell and shut the main door that separated his office from the jail cells.

Joseph made himself comfortable on the cot that was provided. He didn't say very much when his evening meal was brought to him. Then he slept that night in the cell and the Sheriff let him out the next afternoon with a warning.

Kurt sat the boys down and explained to them about Joseph Carlyle. He wanted everyone in the family to be aware of how dangerous Joseph could be.

Sam turned up information on Joseph. He reported that Joseph had been in Jefferson City checking out the family for over a month. He found out that he hired Thadeus Conner to approach Kurt with the phony building project. He also found out from Lia and the other girls at the Men's Club that Joseph was trying to find someone who might be angry or upset with Kurt and Ethan.

Sam took Kurt outside away from the house. "Kurt, Lia told me that this guy is obsessed about Lacey. He talks to the girls about her all the time when he is drunk. Lia wanted you to know that he referred to her as Lacey more than once. Lia thinks he has a screw loose."

"I'd like to know how he found us." Kurt said.

"Uncle Kurt, you'd better get in here. Aunt Lacey doesn't look so good." Ed told him.

Kurt came inside and saw Gus helping me to lie down on the couch. "Lacey honey, what's wrong?"

"Just dizzy and my stomach is upset." I told him.

He picked me up and carried me upstairs to our bed. He put me down on it. "It's getting late anyway, maybe you should just go to sleep now."

"Kurt, sit down a minute." I patted the bed so he would sit down next to me.

"Do you want me to stay with you until you fall asleep?" He asked.

"Kurt, I'm pretty sure that I'm pregnant." I smiled at him.

"Really?" He was surprised.

"Yes, and I have some more good news. I'm pretty sure Tricia is too." I told him.

"Does Ethan know?" He asked me.

"We planned on telling you both tonight, so I'm pretty sure he knows now. Surprise." I told him.

He kissed me. "Did you see the doctor yet?"

"No, but I will soon. I'm fine except for being a little dizzy and sick to my stomach." I told him.

"Well, with everything going on like it is, I'm not leaving you home alone." He insisted.

"You need the boys on the job. I know what a big project you and Ethan are working on. Gus can't stay home every day." I told him.

"I know that, but for now he is going to. Ethan is bringing Tricia here in the morning to keep you company. You can knit booties for the babies together and I'll give Gus some chores to take care of around the house and in the barn. He'll be close by if you need him. I'll check on you at lunch time." Kurt said.

I stayed afraid for about a week and then I started to get angry about Joseph invading the peace of my life and disrupting my family. I started to do a little checking of my own and decided to find a way to visit Joseph by myself. It took a bit of maneuvering but I got Kurt to drop me off at Tricia's house one morning. When she nodded off to sleep I took her buggy into town and found Joseph's home. I knocked on the door.

He smiled when he opened the door to me. "This is a pleasant surprise."

"Can I come in Joseph?" I asked him.

"By all means." He invited me.

I sat down on his couch and he stood against his fireplace waiting for me to speak.

"What exactly are you after Joseph?" I asked him.

"You know Lacey, I always thought of you as a kind of timid person and now you show up at my home and boldly ask me what I am after. I must say, I am delightfully surprised by the change in your personality." He said.

"Answer the question Joseph. You traveled a long way and went through a great amount of trouble to come here. Why are you here?" I asked him again.

"I came for vengeance." He said.

"Vengeance for what?" I asked him.

"Dear sweet Lacey, you crushed my plans to have you as my wife." He knelt down in front of me and looked directly into my eyes. "I had plans for us. You are lovelier than anyone I've ever met. I thought about you day and night when you boarded that ship and left for England. I couldn't persuade myself to think of another. Then I thought I had another chance to make you my wife, but you wouldn't have me again. I've gotten everything I've ever wanted in life. I was spoiled by my parents. They told me that nothing would be impossible for me. They were wrong. Having you accept me as a husband seemed impossible until I devised that plan on the island. Once again I thought I would hold you in my arms and kiss your lips and make you in every sense my very own. You burned my hopes again and left me standing in that church. Do you know that I think of you even now? At this moment I smell the sweet scent of your hair and I want your lips to be pressed against mine. I want to feel the softness of your neck." He leaned toward me and I moved away and stood up.

"Is that your goal? You just came here to have something that you can never have? I won't leave my husband. I love him. I couldn't marry you. I never loved you. If I ever led you to believe that was a possibility then I apologize. You have to stop this pursuit. There will never be a time that you and I will share anything. Please get on with your life Joseph and find someone who can love you in return. I'm not as wonderful as you have imagined. Find someone who is better suited to you and leave me and my family alone." I tried to insist.

He immediately wrapped his arms around me. "I could have you right here Lacey. You came to see me in my house. They would believe that you initiated this romantic moment." He pressed the side of his face against mine and whispered in my ear. "I can feel your heart beating against my chest. Do you feel the excitement of this moment Lacey? You are not so sure that when my lips touch yours you won't want to give yourself to me. That is why you fight to be free, isn't it? Breathe Lacey. I love the sound of your breathing." He whispered.

"Open this door or I will break it down!" Came the voice of my husband as he pounded on the door. "Open the door!"

"Ah Lacey, saved once again." He let go of me and went to his front door and opened it to Kurt. "Good morning Mr. Albert. You must be looking for your lovely wife."

Kurt was red with anger. "Lacey, get in the buggy." Kurt walked in and got behind me. Then he escorted me out of Joseph's house.

"I'll see you soon." Joseph called after me and shut his door.

I climbed into the buggy with Kurt's help. My hands were shaking as I took the reins.

"Go home now." He ordered.

I drove the buggy home and he followed me. He helped me out of the buggy and pointed to the front door. Then he followed me inside.

"I have left Gus with you for over a week." He slammed the front door. "I've made sure Tricia was with you each day and the minute you get the chance you go off and visit the guy? What is wrong with you? Why would you take such a chance and go into his house?" He yelled.

I was shaking with nervousness. "I was tired of being a prisoner in my own home. He has disrupted our lives. I wanted to confront him and find out what he was after." I tried to keep myself from crying as I explained.

"He is after you! He wants you Lacey and you made yourself available to him in his own home. Didn't you consider how dangerous that would be for you? He is bigger than you and certainly stronger. What you did was stupid. You put yourself and the baby in danger. You waved yourself in front of him and dared him not to touch you."

"I did not!" I turned away from him.

"Yes Lacey, you did. He knows that you went there without my knowledge or permission. In essence you showed him that you don't have to tell me anything." Kurt insisted.

I turned back to face him. "I wasn't trying to give him that impression. I just wanted to confront him and stop this somehow. I thought if I reasoned with him and showed him that I wasn't afraid of him, that he would leave us alone."

"And what happened?" Kurt asked. "Did you get the results you wanted?"

I didn't want to tell him. I ran up to our bedroom to get away from the conversation and he ran up after me.

"What happened Lacey?" He grabbed my arm and spun me around to face him.

I started to cry.

"Lacey, your tears are not going to stop this conversation. What happened? What was the result of your act of boldness?" He persisted.

"I was wrong. He wanted me and he would have taken me if you hadn't shown up when you did." I cried.

"Did he touch you?" Kurt asked me and when I wouldn't answer he shook me. "Did he touch you?" He yelled.

"He held me in his arms. He let me know what was going

to happen, but he didn't have the chance to do any of it. You came and rescued me." I cried.

Kurt put his arms around me and held me close to him while I cried. "Lacey, you have no idea what he is capable of. He has no conscience and no regard for your marriage to me. You've tied my hands. I can't go after him because you went to see him in his own house. I would like nothing better than to beat him into unconsciousness, but I can't even do that now. He will use this meeting against you and against us."

"I'm so sorry. I'm so sorry Kurt. I didn't think ahead. I didn't see any of this. I thought that if I talked with him and told him how much I loved you he would leave us alone. I thought if I showed him I wasn't afraid of him, he would back away. I was stupid and naïve. I'm so sorry." I apologized through my tears.

"Come sit down on the bed." He took me gently to the bed and sat beside me. "You're safe Lacey. Please stop crying. I'm sorry I was so rough with you. I shouldn't have shaken you like that. I lost my temper and I shouldn't have treated you like that. I'm very sorry. I promise that will not happen again. No matter how upset I am with you, you're my wife and you deserve to be treated better than that. I'm very sorry."

"He frightened me Kurt. What can we do now? I've made things worse." I was so worried.

We heard someone knocking on our front door.

"Lacey, lie down and rest. I'll go see who it is." Kurt said. He left me in the bedroom and went to the door.

I heard him open the door and crack up laughing. I got up and went to the top of the staircase and looked through the railing to the front door. Kurt was still laughing at this beautiful woman who was wearing a blue dress and blue hat with big white feathers in it. She was carrying a piece of luggage and a purse.

I heard her say, "Well Mr. Albert, aren't you going to invite me in?"

He motioned for her to come in and he just kept laughing. I walked down the staircase to the parlor and the woman walked to greet me.

"So glad to make your acquaintance Mrs. Albert." She said politely.

Kurt was still laughing. "Lacey, that is no lady."

"I beg your pardon." The woman turned around indignantly and addressed my husband.

I didn't understand what was so funny. Then Kurt came over to stand beside me.

"Lacey honey, this is my good friend Ted Clayborn. One of his many talents in life is being able to disguise himself and act the part. His other talents include gambling and scheming." Kurt explained.

Ted removed his hat and wig. "Hi Lacey."

I stood there in shock. He spoke like a man.

"Kurt, help me out here. I need a place to clean up and change out of these clothes." He said.

"Sure, follow me." Kurt directed him to Ed's room. "There is a pitcher of clean water and soap on the bureau. Come back out when you are yourself again." Kurt closed the door to the bedroom and returned to me. "I have no idea how he found us. I haven't seen him since we left England. We were great friends. He got me into and out of a lot of trouble."

When he came out of the bedroom he looked totally different. He was quite handsome and had muscular arms, but he was short for a man, about my size. I just couldn't believe it was the same person.

"Now I feel like myself again. Really Lacey, I have no idea how you women stand all that fluff and maintenance." He said as he sat down at our dining room table to join us.

"How did you find us?" Kurt asked.

"A man by the name of Prentice Sheffield pointed me in the right direction. He actually hired me to come here and help you out. Seems you should be expecting a problem from someone called Joseph Carlyle." Ted explained.

"He is already here and already a problem." Kurt said. "How did Prentice know where to send you and that Carlyle was going to be a problem for us?" Kurt asked.

"I wrote to Prentice and gave him our address." I explained.

"When did you do that?" Kurt asked.

"Over three months ago." I answered.

"Mr. Sheffield discovered a spy for Joseph Carlyle was

working for him. The woman in question gave him the information he needed to track you down. When Sheffield discovered the leak he sent for me. I'm here to help. Just tell me what the problem is and I'll do my best to take care of it." Ted offered.

"How did Mr. Sheffield know about you? I never mentioned you to him." Kurt asked.

"I have a good reputation in England for doing a specific kind of work. When Sheffield hired me he had no idea that I already knew who you were. I haven't filled him in on that either. I didn't want to lower my price. So I get to visit my old friend and help out and I get paid for it." Ted explained.

"Lacey, can you get us some coffee and something to eat?" Kurt asked.

"Sure." I got up from the table to make the coffee.

"Ted, let's take a walk. Lacey, I just want a few minutes alone with Ted." Kurt said as they walked to the front door.

"Alright." I replied as I watched them walk outside.

"What's up?" Ted asked.

"I know how you operate. You take chances and I'm telling you that whatever you decide to do to help us out, none of it can come back on this family. Stay away from anything illegal, no stealing, no killing, and no physical harm that would land anyone in jail." Kurt warned him.

Ted smiled. "I understand. Now tell me what is going on with this guy who wanted to hunt you down."

"He is obsessed with my wife. He proposed to her in England. He comes from a very wealthy family and treated her well while they were in England. Then he asked her to marry him and she turned him down. She told him it was because her family was moving to America and she was going with them. I met Lacey on the ship. There was a storm and the ship went down. Only Lacey and her brother Ethan survived it along with Tricia and me. We washed up on an island and Prentice Sheffield took us in. Joseph Carlyle's family lived on the island too. Joseph was visiting his parents on the island and found out Lacey was there. He tried to start up the relationship again without success. We thought he had just given up. Lacey and I were getting close to each other and we thought Carlyle had gotten that message. He ended up trying to blackmail her into marrying him. He threatened to have her brother Ethan taken back to England to stand trial for a crime he didn't commit. We escaped the island and got married. We changed our names so we wouldn't have a problem in America. I guess when he intercepted our address he decided to pursue Lacey here. He has already been locked up once as a warning, but this morning my wife got the brilliant idea to confront him at his home. It didn't go well at all. If I hadn't shown up when I did to rescue her, you would be visiting me in jail and Carlyle wouldn't be a problem for anyone right now." Kurt explained.

"Wow. I guess I'm going to need a few days to check out this guy and find his weak link." Ted said as they walked.

"You can stay here as long as it takes. I could use some hope and I know Lacey could." Kurt said.

"I'll stay the night, but in the morning I'll get a room at the hotel in town. I don't want Carlyle to put us together when I am trying to butter him up." Ted said.

"Whatever you need, you just let me know." Kurt offered.

"Right now I need a coffee and some food." Ted smiled.

Chapter Eleven

Over the next few weeks we saw very little of Ted. Kurt informed us that Ted had met Joseph as himself and played poker with him on numerous occasions. He had informed Kurt that he was devising a fool proof plan and that when the time came to implement it he would need everyone's cooperation and patience. Kurt inquired about the specifics of the plan, but Ted wouldn't share any of it yet.

About six weeks later a ship called *Seven Seas* pulled into the Harbor of Jefferson City. It wasn't in very good shape, but the Captain claimed it was sea worthy. Ted was very interested in the ship. He convinced the Captain to give him a tour of it. He talked to the Captain about a business deal that might bring in a good deal of money. The Captain seemed very interested. Ted spent the next seven days going over the specifics of the deal with him, swearing him to secrecy.

Joseph Carlyle had noticed the relationship Ted seemed to have with the Captain. He was curious about it. After their usual poker game Joseph inquired about it when they were sitting alone drinking whiskey.

"I notice you spend a lot of time on the *Seven Seas*." Joseph said.

"I'm the type of man who is always looking for a deal. I like making money, you know that." Ted said.

"Yes, you seem to gravitate toward the pot of gold." Joseph smiled. "Have you been working on the issues we discussed?"

"Be patient Joseph. I like planning every detail. I assure you that you didn't approach me about your particular situation in vain." Ted told him.

"I want that whole family to pay for keeping Lacey from me. You just make sure that I leave here with her in my arms." Joseph said.

"That's the plan." Ted smiled. "You are aware she is pregnant."

"Yes I've heard the news. I have no intention of harming my future child. Lacey and I will live together in every sense as man and wife raising our little one together. The baby will be my insurance that she will not leave me again." Joseph told him.

"You must really love this girl." Ted said.

"Beyond anything you could imagine." Joseph told him.

"I've arranged passage for you on the *Seven Seas* when it pulls out of here next week, but it will cost you for the plans I've made." Ted told him.

"Fill me in." Joseph said.

"I've arranged for Ed and Gus Albert to be kidnapped and taken on board as the Captain's new crew. They will be tied up below deck until we are sure that they get the message that there will be no escape. I will arrange for Kurt to be inaccessible to Lacey. I will bring her to the ship to speak to the Captain about setting her nephews free. When he insists that she come below and identify them, the Captain will take her below and lock her away. Then he will cast off." Joseph leaned back in his chair and looked proud of himself. "After that you can take her. Just threaten to have her nephews thrown overboard and she will give you whatever you wish. The Captain will drop you off wherever you like and he will take the boys like intended. The family you wanted destroyed will be destroyed and you and Lacey can live happily ever after. Kurt will have no idea where to find his wife or his nephews. I will play the part of the concerned friend and after a time I will walk away and spend the cash you paid me to set this up. How is that for a plan?" Ted smiled.

"I like it. What day are you planning this for?" Joseph asked.

"You have to be hidden away on board with all your stuff on Wednesday morning. The Captain will take you on board just before sunrise. That way no one will see you. He has arranged for a cabin for you and Lacey." Ted said.

"And the boys?" Joseph asked.

"Already on board. Kurt will be desperately looking for the boys and I'll send him, Ethan, and Sam off in the wrong direction. Then I'll come back and get Lacey to come to the ship to rescue them. There will be no mistakes." Ted assured him.

"I like your style. I'm so glad I took the time to get you

here. Are you sure you have no hidden loyalty to Kurt?" Joseph asked.

"I go where the money takes me. The plan to get me here was a good one. I will deliver what you want. I value my reputation as a man who can make things happen. My reputation is my income, no loyalty stands above that." Ted told him.

They shook on it.

"Pay me the money for your passage and for all the accommodations the Captain is making for you. He is taking a big risk. He plans on casting off as soon as Lacey is locked away. Our deal is that you stay out of sight, but you can see Lacey get on the ship from where the Captain will put you. After they cast off you can take her. That's the deal." Ted said.

"I'm not a man who takes chances. I'll be watching this unfold. Where are you taking the boys from?" Joseph asked.

"The livery, Tuesday night. You can watch from your hotel room window. The boys will be stuffed into barrels and loaded on the ship. I have four men meeting me at the livery at eight o'clock Tuesday night. They will be carrying the barrels to the ship." Ted explained.

"How are you going to get them there?" Joseph asked.

"I will have to plan as I go, but they will be there. You just make sure you are on that ship before sunrise." Ted said.

"I'll be there." Joseph said.

Chapter Twelve

Tuesday evening Joseph watched from his hotel room window and saw the four men from the ship carrying two large barrels. They disappeared behind the livery stable and out of sight. A few minutes later Ted showed up with Ed and Gus. About twenty minutes later he saw Ted say goodbye to the men as they rolled the two large barrels containing the boys back toward the ship. When no one was around he went out of the hotel and into the livery stable to make sure Ed and Gus were not hiding inside. He was satisfied that Ted had made good on his plan so he went to the Men's Club to make sure he had an alibi for the evening.

Kurt showed up around eleven o'clock with Sam. He stormed over to the table where Joseph was playing cards with three other men. "Where did you put my boys?" Kurt accused him.

Joseph looked up at the angry man. "I'm not interested in your boys. I have no idea where they are, nor do I care. Maybe you should check the rooms. They are coming of age you know."

Kurt turned over a chair as he approached the bartender. "Has he been here all night?" Kurt asked about Joseph.

"Yeah, right there for hours just like every other night." The bartender told him.

"What time did he come in?" Kurt asked.

"Seven or eight o'clock." The bartender answered.

"Have you seen two young boys hanging around? They are around sixteen years old." Kurt asked.

"No not tonight." He answered.

Lia came over to him. "Hi Kurt. Hi Sam. You look upset. Is there something I can help you with?"

"Have you seen Ed and Gus? Can you check with the other girls?" Kurt asked.

"Sure, I'll check. I haven't seen them, but wait here and I'll check." Lia left them and went to track down all the girls. She returned a few minutes later. "No one has seen them. I'm sorry Kurt. Do they have girlfriends in the area?"

"No one who would be out this late. Thanks Lia." Kurt said as he turned to leave.

"Well, I'll keep my ears open. I'll check with the customers through the night. If I hear anything I'll get word to you." She said.

Kurt made eye contact with Ted on his way out. He wanted him to come outside and talk to him. Ted waited about ten minutes after Kurt left and he threw in his cards.

"Time to call it a night gentlemen. Thanks for the game." Ted left the Men's Club and headed for the hotel.

Kurt grabbed him by the shirt and yanked him around to the back of the hotel. "Is this part of your plan? Are you in on this somehow?"

"In on what? I'm working for you not against you. Tell me what you need and I'll do it, but don't let your anger blow this. Joseph can't find out we know each other." Ted told him.

"My boys are missing. I want them back." Kurt told him.

"I'll be at your place in the morning. I can't get away now. If I hear anything I'll let you know." Ted promised.

"Come on Sam. We won't find them tonight." Kurt let go of Ted and they left to return home.

The next morning Joseph boarded the ship before sunrise. The Captain told him where he could look out and watch the events. "Come this way Mr. Carlyle and I will show you where you and the lady will be staying." Then he opened the door to the room.

"I want to see the boys." Joseph insisted as he peeked into the room.

"What boys?" The Captain asked. "If I had boys on my ship I could get in a lot of trouble, so as far as you are concerned I have no boys. Do we understand each other?"

"Will Lacey Albert be shown the boys you don't have?" He asked.

"As soon as we cast off I will show her what I have." He said.

"That's good enough for me." Joseph smiled and returned

to his vantage point to watch the events unfold.

Ted was at Kurt's house early. "I've got some news. There were some gypsies going through the edge of town yesterday. Someone said he saw the boys hanging around them last night. My information says they were headed south out of town. They could be as much as six hours ahead of you. They have three wagons. You'll all need to go. I can watch over Lacey and Tricia at a distance. I can keep Joseph away from them until you return." Ted promised.

"Alright. Sam and I will get Ethan and send Tricia back here to stay with Lacey. You promise to protect her?" Kurt asked.

"You have my word." Ted promised.

An hour later two men showed up at the ship. They approached the Captain. "Tell Mr. Carlyle that his information is correct, we confirmed it."

The Captain relayed the message and Joseph sent him back to the men with a cash reward for checking out Ted's plan.

Ted disappeared for thirty minutes and then came back to me before Tricia got to the house. "Lacey, I found the boys."

"You did! That's wonderful!" I told him.

"Not really. They were kidnapped last night by the Captain and crew of the *Seven Seas*. He is due to leave the harbor in less than an hour with the boys." Ted explained.

"I'll get the sheriff." I told him.

"You can't risk it. If he sees the sheriff he could kill the boys and dump their bodies into the water. You have to come with me. I have a plan." Ted said.

I got into my buggy and he followed me with his horse to the hotel. He took me to his room. Ed and Gus were waiting for me when I entered the room.

"Boys!" I hugged them. "We've been so worried about you. I don't understand. Ted what is going on?"

"Joseph Carlyle hired me to betray you. It wasn't Prentice Sheffield that got me here. I just told you that. I had every intention of helping Joseph until I got to know your family and I remembered that my friendship with Kurt meant more to me than the money. So I started to set Joseph Carlyle up. The rest of this plan is on me and you are going to have to smooth things over between me and Kurt when he gets back tonight. I sent someone after him to retrieve him, but I needed him out of this. I was being watched and my plan had to look legitimate. Now it's time to become Lacey Albert. Lacey change into this dress and give me your clothes. Boys, hold this blanket up and give Lacey some privacy. We have to make this quick." Ted instructed.

He was quick to apply his disguise. He looked like a mirror image of me. The boys and I were amazed at the likeness.

"You all stay here for at least an hour. Wait ten minutes before you peak out the window to watch the harbor. Make sure no one spots you looking out this window or you might get me killed. Make sure the *Seven Seas* has pulled away from the dock and then wait another thirty minutes before you head for home. Try not to be noticed. Wish me luck." Ted said.

Then he left us.

He got into my buggy and drove it to the ship. He made a fuss with the Captain about the boys. He demanded the Captain let him inspect the ship. The Captain played his part well and took Ted by the hand as Joseph watched. Joseph was convinced that I had stepped into his trap as the ship pulled away from the dock.

We waited thirty minutes and then Ed arranged for someone from the hotel to bring our buggy back from the dock and around to the back of the hotel. We left for home as soon as the young man returned to us. Ed paid him for his service and his silence.

Tricia had let herself into the house and was frantic with worry about where I had gone. She hugged all of us when we entered the house. We explained that it was all part of Ted's plan. About six hours later Kurt and Sam returned to the house with Ethan. The boys explained that Ted convinced them to cooperate with him and that he hid them under hay and horse manure so that Joseph wouldn't find them in the livery. Then I explained what I knew.

"So no one knows the end of this plan?" Kurt asked.

"No, Ted didn't tell us." I told him.

It was over a week before we saw Ted again. He came knocking on our door while we were sitting down for supper. Kurt opened the door to his smiling face.

"Well, Mr. Carlyle won't be bothering you again." Ted said.

"Come in and join us. I can't wait to hear your story." Kurt invited him in.

The boys got up and shook his hand and I got up and hugged him.

"I'm so glad you are safe." I told him.

"Me too." He said. Then he sat down to join us. "I'm starving." He was dressed as himself.

"What happened?" Kurt asked.

"Well, I'm sure Lacey and the boys filled you in on their part all the way to the time of my leaving them. I'm sorry Kurt that I had to do it the way I did, but I needed you to act the part. I wasn't sure you would be able to be convincing if you knew the plan." Ted said.

"I get that. I'm not as good at making it seem realistic as you are." Kurt admitted. "What happened?"

"The Captain kept me away from Joseph until we were in the middle of the river with little view of land. The sun was already going down. Then he let Joseph visit me in his cabin. Joseph was unaware of my particular talent at becoming a female. I keep that to myself and it has proven to protect me at times. I kept my face turned away from him most of the time. I told him that I didn't want to look on the face of the man who had hurt my family so much. He confessed his undying love and protection and then he threatened to have the boys killed if I didn't cooperate. I refused his advances and he ordered the Captain to throw the boys overboard. I screamed that neither of them knew how to swim. The

Captain played his part so well. He was a lunatic. He wanted quiet and cooperation so he went right out and threw the boys overboard. Of course neither of us saw that happen. We just heard the splash and he came back and told Joseph it was done. Joseph was shocked that the Captain had been so quick to follow his orders. I screamed that he was now responsible for the death of two people that I loved dearly and I broke free from the room and ran through the upper deck. I stumbled and fell overboard. Actually I threw myself overboard, but he didn't recognize the truth. I'm very talented. His dear beloved Lacey drowned as the ship continued on its journey." Ted explained.

We all cracked up laughing.

"How did he not know it was you?" Sam asked.

"The room had barely any light and it was dark outside." Ted explained as he spoke just like me.

"You can mimic my voice?" I was amazed.

"Of course I can. I spent weeks listening to you. Kurt will tell you that I can mimic most people. It's a gift." He smiled.

"It's true, if you hang around with him long enough he can sound just like any of you." Kurt said.

"How did you make it to shore if you were so far from it?" Ed asked.

"The Captain had already dropped a rope off the side of the ship. It was too dark for anyone to find me and he made sure to shine the lanterns away from me. After Joseph gave up and returned to his cabin the crew pulled me back up. I cleaned up and the Captain let me off at the next harbor unnoticed. I paid him for his silence and he left a few hours later with Joseph Carlyle grieving the loss, still on board." Ted explained.

"How do you know the Captain won't give you away and explain all this to Joseph?" Kurt asked.

"He's really a nice guy. He has a family of his own and a daughter about Lacey's age. I explained the situation and he was more than happy to help. He didn't really want my money, but a deal is a deal. So right now I'm broke and I haven't got a place to stay. Any suggestions?" He asked.

Kurt laughed. "You can stay with us and you'll have a job as long as you want it."

"I figure I'll be here a few months and then I'll move on to greener pastures. I like what I do and people are always looking for a scoundrel to tie up their messes." He said.

We finished the evening meal and sat around enjoying the company of our friend. Ed moved in with Gus and Ted took over Ed's bedroom.

Kurt climbed into bed next to me. "I had no idea when I started out from England that I would be responsible for so many people."

"Some day it will be just you and me and the baby." I told him.

"I doubt that Lacey." He rubbed my belly. "We have a lot of bedrooms here. When all these young men find a place of their own, I plan on filling those rooms with our children."

"Do you really?" I smiled.

"I've got lots of love and attention to give and I don't want to overwhelm you with it. You couldn't handle that much love and attention. I'm only thinking of your well being." He joked.

I laughed. "Really, you have that much?"

"Absolutely, I've been rationing you since we got married. If I poured out all my love and attention in your direction you would be running after me all the time, craving me like your favorite meal." He kissed me.

"I think you are all talk." I smiled.

"Oh so you want proof, do you?" He tightened his loving embrace of me.

"Yes I do. Prove to me that you're not all talk. Go ahead start tonight, I can take it." I dared him.

"Alright Lacey Albert, from now on I'm not holding back to protect you from this overwhelming experience of love and attention. You just remember this night was a turning point in our relationship and you are the one who wanted this. When you start chasing after me in public I'm not running away. When you beg to shower me with your attention and beg me for affection I'm not turning you down. It won't matter what time of the day it is or where we are. You remember that." He sounded serious.

I whispered. "I promise, my heart will remember all of this." Then I kissed him.

ABOUT THE AUTHOR

    Cheryl OBrien has written twenty one books since April of 2013. Lacey is her twenty-first book. Her desire is to encourage the reader to believe that strong women do exist as do honorable men and to hold out for God's best.   Her other books include
Katie's Journey Series (5 books)
Kelly, Samantha, Emily, Serena, Gina, Elaine
Sarah Tilly
Miranda Cove
On That Day
Jenna and Jenna's Flame
Secrets and Love
Jack and Roxanne
My King
You Were Chosen
    Check them out on Amazon.com by typing in Cheryl OBrien Books

Made in the USA
Charleston, SC
25 May 2014